# THE PLANET EXPLORER

# MORE WILDSIDE CLASSICS

# THE PLANET EXPLORER

# MURRAY LEINSTER

**WILDSIDE PRESS**

# THE PLANET EXPLORER

# I

## SOLAR CONSTANT

Bordman waked that morning when the partly-opened port of his sleeping-cabin closed of itself and the room-warmer began to whir. He found himself burrowed deep under his covering, and when he got his head out of it the already-bright room was bitterly cold and his breath made a fog about his head.

He thought uneasily *it's colder than yesterday!* But a Senior Colonial Survey Officer is not supposed to let himself seem disturbed in public, and the only way to follow that rule is to follow it in private too. So Bordman composed his features, while gloom filled him. When one has just received senior service rating and is on one's very first independent survey of a new colonial installation, the unexpected can be appalling. The unexpected was definitely here, on Lani III.

He'd been a Survey Candidate on Khali II and Taret and Arepo I, all of which were tropical, and a Junior Officer on Menes III and Thotmes — one a semi-arid planet and the other temperate-volcanic — and he'd done an assistant job on Saril's solitary world, which was nine-tenths water. But this first independent survey on his own was another matter. Everything was wholly unfamiliar. An ice planet with a minus point one habitability rating was upsetting in its peculiarities. He knew what the books said about glacial-world conditions, but that was all.

The denseness of the fog his breath made seemed to grow less as the room-warmer whirred and whirred. When by the thinness of the mist he guessed the temperature to be not much under freezing, he climbed out of his bunk and went to the port to look out. His cabin, of course, was in one of the drone-hulls that had brought the colony's equipment to Lani III. The other emptied hulls were precisely ranged in order outside. They were connected by tubular galleries, and painstakingly leveled. They gave the impression of impassioned tidiness among the upheaved, ice-coated mountains all about.

He gazed down the long valley in which the colony lay. There were monstrous slanting peaks on either side that partly framed the morning sun. Their flanks were ice. The sky was pale, and the sun had four sun-dogs geometrically about it. Normally post-midnight temperatures in this valley ranged from ten below zero Fahrenheit— and this was technically summer. But it was colder than ten degrees below zero now. At noon there were normally tiny trickling rills of surface-thaw running down the sunlit sides of the mountains, but they froze again at night. And this was a sheltered valley, warmer than most of the planet's surface. The sun had its sun-dogs every day, on rising. There were nights when the brighter planets had star-pups, too.

The phone-plate lighted and dimmed and lighted and dimmed. They did themselves well on Lani III; the parent world was in this same solar system, making supply easy. That was rare. Bordman stood before the plate and it cleared. Herndon's face peered unhappily out of it. He was even younger than Bordman, and inclined to lean on the supposedly vast experience of a Senior Officer of the Colonial Survey.

"Well?" said Bordman, feeling undignified in his sleeping garments.

"We're picking up a beam from home," said Herndon anxiously. "But we can't make it out."

Because the third planet of the sun Lani was being colonized from the second, inhabited world, communication with the colony's base was possible. A tight beam could span a distance which was only light-minutes across at conjunction, and not much over a light-hour at opposition, as now. But the beam communication had been broken for the past few weeks, and should be possible again for some weeks more. The sun lay between. One wouldn't expect normal sound-and-picture transmission until the parent planet had moved past the scrambler-fields of Lani. But something had come through. It would be reasonable for it to be pretty much hash when it arrived.

"They aren't sending words or pictures," said Herndon. "The beam is wobbly and we don't know what to make of it. It's a signal, all right, and on the regular frequency. But there are all sorts of stray noises and still in the midst of it there's some sort of signal we can't make out. It's like a whine, only it stutters. It's a broken-up sound of one pitch."

Bordman rubbed his chin. He remembered a course in information theory just before he graduated from the Service Academy. Signals were made by pulses, pitch-changed, and frequency-variations. Information was what couldn't be predicted without information. And he remembered with gratitude a seminar on the history of communication, just before he'd gone out on his first field job as a Survey Candidate.

"Hm," he said with a trace of self-consciousness. "Those noises, the stuttering ones. Would they be, on the whole, of no more than two different durations? Like — hm. — *Bzz bzz bzzzzzzz bzz?*"

He felt that he lost dignity by making such ribald sounds. But Herndon's face brightened.

"That's it!" he said relievedly. "That's it! Only they're high-pitched like —" His voice went falsetto. "Bz bz bz bzzz bz bz."

Bordman thought, *we sound like idiots.* He said:

"Record everything you get, and I'll try to decode it." He added, "Before there was voice communication, there were signals of light and sound in code which rendered words. Very crude system, but it worked when there was a lot of interference, as in the early days. If there's some emergency, your home world might try to get through the sun's scrambled-field that way."

"Undoubtedly!" said Herndon, with even great relief. "No question, that's it!"

He regarded Bordman with respect as he clicked off. His image faded.

*He thinks I'm wonderful,* thought Bordman wryly. *Because I'm Colonial Survey. But all I know is what's been taught me. It's bound to show up sooner of later. Damn!*

He dressed. From time to time he looked out the port again. The intolerable cold of Lani III had intensified, lately. There was some idea that sunspots were the cause. He couldn't make out sunspots with the naked eye, but the sun did look pale, with its accompanying sun-dogs, the result of microscopic ice-crystals suspended in the air. There was no dust on this planet, but there was plenty of ice! It was in the air and on the ground and even under it. To be sure, the drills for the foundation of the great landing-grid had brought up cores of frozen humus along with frozen clay, so there must have been a time when this world had known clouds and seas and vegetation. But it was millions, maybe hundreds of millions of years ago. Right now, though, it was only warm enough to have an atmosphere and very slight and partial thawings in direct sunlight, in sheltered spots, at midday. It couldn't support life, and there is a temperature below which a natural ecological system can't maintain itself. And for the past few weeks, the climate had been such that even human-supplied life looked dubious.

Bordman slipped on his Colonial Survey uniform with its palm-tree insignia. Nothing could be much more inappropriate that palm-tree symbols on a planet with sixty feet of permafrost, Bordman reflected. *The construction gang calls it a blast, instead of a tree, because we blow up when they try to dodge specifications. But specifications have to be met! You can't bet the lives of a colony or even a ship's crew on half-built facilities!*

He marched down the corridor from his sleeping-room, with the dignity he tried to maintain for the sake of the Colonial Survey. It was a pretty lonely business, being dignified all the time. If Herndon didn't look so respectful it would have been pleasant to be more friendly. But Herndon revered him. Even his sister Riki . . .

But Bordman put her firmly out of his mind. He was on Lani III, which had very valuable mineral resources that made colonization worthwhile, to check and approve the colony installations. There was the giant landing-grid for spaceships, which took power from the ionosphere to bring space vessels gently to the ground, and also to supply the colony's power needs. It likewise lifted visiting spacecraft the necessary five planetary diameters out when they took off again. There was power storage in the remote event of disaster to that giant device. There was a food reserve and the necessary resources for its indefinite stretching in case of need. That usually meant hydroponic installations. All these things had had to be finished, operable, and inspected by a duly qualified Colonial Survey officer before the colony could be licensed for unlimited use.

It was all very normal and official, but Bordman was the newest Senior Survey Officer on the list, and this was the first of his independent operations. He felt inadequate at times.

He passed through the vestibule between this drone-hull and the next and went directly to Herndon's office. Herndon, like himself, was newly endowed with authority. He was actually a mining-and-minerals man and a youthful prodigy in that field, but when the director of the colony was taken ill while a supply-ship was aground, he went back to the home planet and command devolved on Herndon. *I wonder*, thought Bordman, *if he feels as shaky as I do.*

When he entered the office, Herndon sat listening to a literal hash of noises coming out of a speaker on his desk. The cryptic signal had been relayed to him, and a recorder stored it as it came. There were cracklings and squeals and moaning sounds, sputters and rumbles and growls. But behind the façade of confusion there was a tiny, interrupted, high-pitched noise. It was a monotone whining not to be confused with the random sounds accompanying it. Sometimes it faded almost to inaudibility, and sometimes it was sharp and clear. But it was a distinctive sound in itself, and it was made up of short whines and longer ones of two durations only.

"I've put Riki at making a transcription of what we've got," said Herndon with relief as he saw Bordman. "She'll make short marks for the short sounds, and long ones for the long. I've told her to try to separate the groups. We've got a full half-hour of it, already."

Bordman made an inspired guess.

"I would expect it to be the same message repeated over and over," he said. He added. "And I think it would be decoded by guessing at the letters in two-letter and three-letter words, as clues to longer ones. That's quicker than statistical analysis of frequency."

Herndon instantly pressed buttons under his phone-plate. He relayed the information to his sister, as if it were gospel. *But it wasn't,* Bordman remembered. *It's simply a trick remembered from boyhood, when I was interested in secret languages. My interest faded when I realized I had no secrets to record or transmit.*

Herndon turned from the phone-plate.

"Riki says she's already learned to recognize some groups," he reported, "but thanks for the advice. Now what?"

Bordman sat down. "It seems to me," be observed, "that the increased cold out here might not be local. Sunspots —"

Herndon wordlessly handed over a sheet of paper with observation figures on top and a graph below them which related the observations to each other. They were the daily, at-first-routine, measurements of the solar constant from Lani III. The graph-line almost ran off the paper at the bottom.

"To look at this," he admitted, "you'd think the sun was going out. Of course it can't be," he added hastily. "Not possibly. But there is an extraordinary number of sunspots. Maybe they'll clear. But meanwhile the amount of heat reaching us is dropping. As far as I know there's no parallel for it. Night temperatures are thirty degrees lower than they should be. Not only here, either, but at all the robot weather-stations that have been spotted around the planet. They average forty below zero minimum, instead of ten. And — there is that terrific lot of sunspots . . ."

Bordman frowned. Sunspots are things about which nothing can be done. Yet the habitability of a borderline planet, anyhow, could very well depend on them. An infinitesimal change in sun-heat can make a serious change in any planet's temperature. In the books, the ancient mother Earth was said to have entered glacial periods through a drop of only three degrees in the planet-wide temperature, and to have been tropic almost to its poles from a rise of only six. It had been guessed that those changes on the planet where humanity began had been caused by a coincidence of sunspot maxima.

Lani III was already glacial to its equator. Sunspots could account for worsening conditions here, perhaps. *That message from the inner planet could be bad,* thought Bordman, *if the solar constant drops and stays down awhile.* But aloud he said:

"There couldn't be a really significant permanent change. Not quickly, anyhow. Lani's a sol-type star, and they aren't variables, though of course any dynamic system like a sun will have cyclic modifications of one sort or another. But they usually cancel out."

He sounded encouraging, even to himself.

There was a stirring behind him; Riki Herndon had come silently into her brother's office. She looked pale. She put some papers down on the desk.

"That's true," she said. "But while cycles sometimes cancel, sometimes they enhance each other. They heterodyne. That's what's happening."

Bordman scrambled to his feet, flushing. Herndon said sharply:

"What? Where'd you get that stuff, Riki?"

She nodded at the sheaf of papers she'd just laid down.

"That's the news from home." She nodded again, to Bordman. "You were right. It was the same message, repeated over and over. And I decoded it like children decode each other's secret messages. I did that to Ken once. He was twelve, and I decoded his diary, and I remember how angry he was that I'd found out he didn't have any secrets."

She tried to smile. But Herndon wasn't listening. He read swiftly. Bordman saw that the under sheets were rows of dots and dashes, painstakingly transcribed and then decoded. There were letters under each group of marks.

Herndon was very white when he'd finished. He handed the sheet to Bordman. Riki's handwriting was precise and clear. Bordman read:

> FOR YOUR INFORMATION THE SOLAR CON-
> STANT IS DROPPING RAPIDLY DUE TO COINCIDENCE
> OF CYCLIC VARIATIONS IN SUNSPOT ACTIVITY WITH
> PREVIOUS UNOBSERVED LONG CYCLES APPARENT-
> LY INCREASING THE EFFECT MAXIMUM IS NOT YET
> REACHED AND IT IS EXPECTED THAT THIS PLANET
> WILL BECOME UNINHABITABLE FOR A TIME AL-
> READY KILLING FROSTS HAVE DESTROYED CROPS IN
> SUMMER HEMISPHERE IT IS IMPROBABLE THAT MORE

THAN A SMALL PART OF THE POPULATION CAN BE SHELTERED AND WARMED THROUGH DEVELOPING GLACIAL CONDITIONS WHICH WILL REACH TO EQUATOR IN TWO HUNDRED DAYS THE COLD CONDITIONS ARE COMPUTED TO LAST TWO THOUSAND DAYS BEFORE NORMAL SOLAR CONSTANT RECURS THIS INFORMATION IS SENT YOU TO ADVISE IMMEDIATE DEVELOPMENT OF HYDROPONIC FOOD SUPPLY AND OTHER PRECAUTIONS MESSAGE ENDS FOR YOUR INFORMATION THE SOLAR CONSTANT IS DROPPING RAPIDLY DUE TO COINCIDENCE OF CYCLIC —

Bordman looked up. Herndon's face was ghastly. Bordman said:

"Kent IV is the nearest world your planet could hope to get help from. A mail liner will make it in two months. Kent IV might be able to send three ships — to get here in two months more. That's no good!"

He felt sick. Human-habited planets are far apart. There is on an average between four and five light-years of distance between suns, two months' spaceship journey apart. And not all stars are Sol-type or have inhabited planets. Colonized worlds are like isolated islands in an unimaginably vast ocean, and the ships that fly between them at thirty light-speeds seem merely to creep. In ancient days on the mother-planet Earth, men sailed for months between ports, in their clumsy sailing-ships. There was no way to send messages faster than they could travel. Nowadays there was little improvement. News of the Lani disaster could not be transmitted. It had to be carried, as between stars, and carriage was slow and response to news of disaster was no faster.

The inner planet, Lani II, had twenty million inhabitants, as against the three hundred people in the colony on Lani III. The outer planet was already frozen, but there would be glaciation on the inner world in two hundred days. Glaciation and human life are practically exclusive. Human beings can survive only so long as food and power hold out, and shelter against really bitter cold cannot be quickly improvised for twenty million people. And, of course, there could be no help on any adequate scale. News of the need for it would travel too slowly. It would take five Earth-years to get a thousand ships to Lani II, and a thousand ships could not rescue more than one percent of the population. But in five years there would not be nearly so many people left alive.

"Our people," said Riki in a thin voice, "all of them . . . Mother and father and the others. All our friends. Home is going to be like that!"

She jerked her head toward a port which let in the frigid colony-world's white daylight.

Bordman was aware of an extreme unhappiness on her account. For himself, of course, the tragedy was less. He had no family, and very few friends. But he could see something that had not occurred to them as yet.

"Of course," he said, "it's not only their trouble. If the solar constant is really dropping like that, things out here will be pretty bad, too. A lot worse than they are now. We'll have to get to work to save ourselves!"

Riki did not look at him. Bordman bit his lips. It was plain that their own fate did not concern them immediately. When one's home world is doomed, one's personal safety seems a trivial matter.

There was silence save for the crackling, confused noised that came out of the speaker on Herndon's desk.

"We," said Bordman, "are right now in the conditions they'll face a good long time from now."

Herndon said dully:

"We couldn't live here without supplies from home. Or even without the equipment we brought. But they can't get supplies from anywhere, and they can't make such equipment for everybody! They'll die!" He swallowed. "They — they know it, too. So they warn us to try to save ourselves because they can't help us any more."

Bordman felt lonely. He could understand that nobody would want to live as the only human alive. Nobody would want to live as a member of the only group of people left alive. And everybody thinks of his home planet as all the world there is. *I don't think that way*, thought Bordman. *But maybe it's the way I'd feel about living if Riki were to die.* It would be natural to want to share any danger or any disaster she faced.

"L-look!" he said, stammering a little. "You don't see! It isn't a case of your living while they die! If your home world becomes like this, what will this be like? We're farther from the sun, colder to start with. Do you think we'll live through anything they can't take? Food supplies or no, equipment or no, do you think we've got a chance? Use your brains!"

Herndon and Riki stared at him. And then some of the strained look left Riki's face and body. Herndon blinked, and said slowly:

"Why, that's so! We were thought to be taking a terrific risk when we came here. But it'll be as much worse here. Of course! We are in the same fix they're in!"

He straightened a little. Color actually came back into his face. Riki managed to smile. And then Herndon said almost naturally:

"That makes things look more sensible. We've got to fight for our lives too! And we've very little chance of saving them. What do we do about it, Bordman?"

The sun was halfway toward mid-day, still attended by its sun-dogs, though they were fainter than at the horizon. The sky was darker. The icy mountain peaks reached skyward, serene and utterly aloof from the affairs of men. The city was a fleet of metal hulks, neatly arranged for the building of the colony. Not far away, the landing-grid stood. It was a gigantic skeleton of steel, rising from legs of unequal length bedded in the hillsides and reaching two thousand feet toward the stars. Human figures, muffled almost past recognition, moved about a catwalk three-quarters of the way up. There was a tiny glittering below where they moved. The men were using sonic ice-breakers to shatter the frost which formed on the framework at night. Falling shards of crystals made a liquid-like flashing. The landing-grid needed to be cleared every ten days or so. Left uncleared, it would aquire an increasingly thick coating of ice, and in time it would collapse. But long before that time it would have ceased to operate, and without its operation there could be no space-travel. Rockets for lifting spaceships were impossibly heavy, for practical use. But the landing-grids could lift them out to the unstressed space where Lawlor drives could work, and draw them to ground with cargoes they couldn't possibly have carried if they'd needed rockets.

Bordman reached the base of the grid on foot. He was dwarfed by the ground-level upright beams. He went through the cold-lock to the small control house at the grid's base.

He nodded to the man on standby as he got out of his muffling garments.

"Everything all right?" he asked.

The standby operator shrugged. Bordman was Colonial Survey. It was his function to find fault, to expose inadequacies in the construction and operation of colony facilities. *It's natural for me to be disliked by men whose work I inspect*, thought Bordman. *If I approve it doesn't mean anything, and if I protest, it's bad.*

"I think," he said, "that there ought to be a change in maximum no-drain voltage. I'd like to check it."

The operator shrugged again. He pressed buttons under a phone-plate.

"Shift to reserve power," he commanded, when a face appeared on the plate. "Gotta check no-drain juice."

"What for?" demanded the face in the plate.

"You-know-who's got ideas," said the grid operator scornfully. "maybe we've been skimping something. Maybe there's some new specification we didn't know about. Maybe something! But shift to reserve power."

The face in the screen grumbled. Bordman swallowed. It was not a Survey officer's privilege to maintain discipline. And anyhow, there was no particular virtue in discipline here and now. He watched the current-demand dial. It stood a little above normal day-drain, which was understandable. The outside temperature was down. There was more power needed to keep the dwellings warm, and there was a lot of power needed in the mine the colony had been formed to exploit. The mine had to be warmed for the men who worked to develop it.

The current-demand needle dropped abruptly, hung steady, and dropped again and again as additional parts of the colony's power uses were switched to reserve. The needle hit bottom and stayed there.

Bordman had to walk about the standby man to get to the voltmeter. It was built around standard, old-fashioned vacuum-tubes, and he tested it. He pushed in the contact plugs, read the no-drain voltage, licked his lips and made a note. He reversed the leads, so it would read backward. He took another reading. He drew in his breath very quietly.

"Now I want the power turned on in sections," he told the operator. "The mine first, maybe. It doesn't matter. But I want to get voltage readings at different power take-offs."

The operator looked pained. He spoke with unnecessary elaboration to the face in the phone-plate, and grudgingly went through the process by which Bordman measured the successive drops in voltage with power drawn from the ionosphere. The current available from a layer of ionized gas is, in effect, the current-flow through a conductor with marked resistance. It is possible to infer a gas's ionization from the current it yields.

The cold-lock door opened. Riki Herndon came in, panting a little.

"There's another message from home," she said sharply. Her voice seemed strained. "They picked up our answering-beam and are giving the information you asked for."

"I'll be along," said Bordman. "I just got some information here."

He got into his cold-garments again, and followed her out of the control-hut.

"The figures from home aren't good," said Riki, when mountains visibly rose on every hand around them. "Ken says they're much worse than he thought. The rate of decline in the solar constant's worse than we figured or could believe."

"I see," said Bordman, inadequately.

"It's absurd!" said Riki angrily. "There've been sunspots and sunspot cycles all along — I learned about them in school. I learned about a four-year and a seven-year cycle, and that there were others. They should have known, they should have calculated in advance! Now they talk about sixty-year cycles coming in with a hundred-and-thirty year cycle to pile up with all the others. . . . What's the use of scientists if they don't do their work right and twenty million people die of it?"

Bordman did not consider himself a scientist, but he winced. Riki lagged as they moved over the slippery ice. Her breath was an intermittent cloud about her shoulders, and there was white frost on the front of her cold-garments. Even so quickly the moisture of her breath congealed.

He held out his hand quickly as she slipped, once.

"But they'll beat it!" said Riki in a sort of angry pride. "They're starting to build more landing-grids, back home. Hundreds of them! Not for ships to land by, but to draw power from the ionosphere! They figure that one ship-size grid can keep nearly three square miles of ground warm enough to live on. They'll roof over the streets of cities and pile snow on top for insulation. Then they'll plant food-crops in the streets and gardens, and do what hydroponic growing they can. They're afraid they can't do it fast enough to save everybody, but they'll try!"

Bordman clenched his hands inside their bulky mittens.

"Well?" demanded Riki. "Won't that do the trick?"

"No."

"Why not?"

"I just took readings on the grid, here. The voltage and the conductivity of the layer we draw power from, both depend on ionization. When the intensity of sunlight drops, the voltage drops and the conductivity drops too. It's harder for less power to flow to the area the grid can tap — and the voltage pressure is lower to drive it."

"Don't say any more!" cried Riki. "Not another word!"

Bordman was silent. They went down the last small slope, and passed the opening of the mine, a great drift which bored straight into the mountain. Looking into it, they saw the twin rows of brilliant roof-lights going toward the heart of the stony monster.

They had almost reached the village when Riki said in a stifled voice:

"How bad is it?"

"Very," admitted Bordman. "We have here the conditions the home planet will have in two hundred days. Originally we could draw less than a fifth the power they count on from a grid on Lani II."

Riki ground her teeth.

"Go on!" she said.

"Ionization here is down ten percent," said Bordman. "That means the voltage is down, somewhat more. A great deal more. And the resistance of the layer is greater. Very much greater. When they need power most, on the home planet, they won't draw more from the grid than we do now. It won't be enough."

They reached the village. There were steps to the cold-lock of Herndon's office-hull. They were ice-free, because like the village walkways they were warmed to keep frost from depositing on them. Bordman made a mental note.

In the cold-lock, the warm air pouring in was almost stifling. Riki said defiantly:

"You might as well tell me now!"

"We usually can draw one-fifth as much power, here, as the same sized grid would yield on your home world," he said. "We are drawing — call it sixty percent of normal. A shade over one-tenth of what they expect to draw when the real cold hits them. Their estimates are nine times too high. One grid won't warm three square miles of city. About a third of one is closer. But —"

"That won't be the worst," said Riki in a choked voice. "Is that right? How much good will a grid do?"

Bordman did not answer.

The inner cold-lock door opened. Herndon sat at his desk, even paler than before, listening to the hash of noises that came out of the speaker. He tapped on the desktop, quite unconscious of the action. He looked almost desperately at Bordman.

"Did she tell you?" he asked in a numb voice. "They hope to save maybe half the population. All the children anyhow. . . ."

"They won't," said Riki bitterly.

"Better go transcribe the new stuff that's come in," said her brother. "We might as well know what it says."

Riki went out of the office. Bordman shed his cold-garments. He said:

"The rest of the colony doesn't know what's up yet. The operator at the grid didn't, certainly. But they have to know."

"We'll post the message on the bulletin board," said Herndon. "I wish I could keep it from them. It's not fun to live with. I — might as well not tell them just yet."

"To the contrary," insisted Bordman. "They've got to know right away! You're going to issue orders and they'll need to understand how urgent they are."

Herndon looked hopeless.

"What's the good of doing anything?" When Bordman frowned, he added: "Seriously, is there any use? You're all right. A Survey Ship's due to take you away. It's not coming because they know there's something wrong, but because your job should be finished by now. But it can't do any good! It would be insane for it to land at home. It couldn't carry away more than a few dozen refugees, and there are twenty million people who're going to die. It might offer to take some of us, but I don't think many of us would go. I wouldn't. I don't think Riki would."

"I don't see —"

"What we've got right here," said Herndon, "is what they're going to have back home. And worse. But there's no chance for us to keep alive here! You are the one who pointed it out. I've been figuring, and the way the solar-constant curve is going — I plotted it from the figures they gave us — it couldn't possibly level out until the oxygen, anyhow, is frozen out of the atmosphere here. We aren't equipped to stand anything like that, and we can't be equipped. There isn't equipment to let us stand it indefinitely! Anyhow, the maximum cold conditions will last two thousand days back home — six Earth-years. And there'll be storage of cold in frozen oceans and piled-up glaciers. It'll be twenty years before home will be back to normal in temperature, and the same here. Is there any point in trying to live — just barely to survive — for twenty years before there'll be a habitable planet to go back to?"

Bordman said irritably:

"Don't be a fool! Doesn't it occur to you that this planet is a perfect experiment station, two hundred days ahead of the home world, where ways to beat the whole business can be tried? If we can beat it here, they can beat it there!"

Herndon said:

"Can you name one thing to try here?"

"Yes," snapped Bordman. "I want the walk-heaters and the

step-heaters outside turned off. They use power to keep walkways clear of frost and door-steps not slippery. I want to save that heat!"

Herndon said, "And when you've saved it, what will you do with it?"

"Put it underground to be used as needed!" Bordman said. "Store it in the mine! I want to put every heating-device we can contrive to work in the mine, to heat the rock. I want to draw every watt the grid will yield and warm up the inside of the mountain while we can draw power to do it with. I want the deepest part of the mine too hot to enter! We'll lose a lot of heat, of course. It's not like storing electric power. But we can store heat now, and the more we store the more will be left when we need it!"

Herndon thought. Presently he stirred slightly.

"Do you know, that is an idea . . ." He looked up. "Back home there was a shale-oil deposit up near the ice-caps. It wasn't economical to mine it. Sot they put heaters down in boreholes and heated up the whole shale deposit. Drill-holes let out the hot oil vapors to be condensed. They got out every bit of oil without disturbing the shale. And then the shale stayed warm for years! Farmers bulldozed soil over it and raised crops with glaciers all around them. That could be done again. They could be storing up heat back home!"

Then he drooped.

"But they can't spare power to warm up the ground under cities. They need all the power they've got to build roofs . . . And it takes time to build grids."

Bordman snapped:

"Yes, if they're building regulation ones. By the time they were finished they'd be useless. The ionization here is dropping already. But they don't need to build grids that will be useless later. They can weave cables together on the ground and hang them in the air by helicopters. They wouldn't hold up a landing ship, for an instant, but they'll draw power right away. They'll even power the helis that hold them up! Of course, they'll have defects; they'll have to come down in high winds, for example. They won't be too dependable. But they can put heat in the ground to come out under roofs, to grow food by, to save lives by. What's the matter with them?"

Herndon stirred again. His eyes ceased to be dull and lifeless.

"I'll give the orders for turning off the sidewalks. And I'll send what you just said back home. They should like it."

He looked respectfully at Bordman.

"I guess you know what I'm thinking right now," he said.

Bordman flushed. He felt that Herndon was unduly impressed. Herndon didn't see that the device wouldn't solve anything. It would merely postpone the effects of a disaster. It could not possibly prevent them.

"It ought to be done," he said. "There'll be other things to be done, too."

"Then when you tell them to me," said Herndon, "they'll get done! I'll have Riki put this into that pulse-code you explained to us and she'll get it off right away."

He stood up.

"I didn't explain the code to her!" insisted Bordman. "She was already translating it when you gave her my suggestion!"

"All right," said Herndon. "I'll get this sent back at once!"

He hurried out of the office. *This*, thought Bordman irritably, *is how reputations are made, I suppose. I'm getting one.* But his own reaction was extremely inappropriate. If the people of Lani II did suspend helicopter-supported grids of wire in the atmosphere, they could warm masses of underground rock and stone and earth. They could establish what were practically reservoirs of life-giving heat under their cities. They could contrive that the warmth from below would rise only as it was needed. *But —*

Two hundred days of conditions corresponding to the colony-planet. Then two thousand days of minimum-heat conditions. Then very, very slow return to normal temperatures, long after the sun was back to its previous brilliance. They couldn't store enough heat for so long. It couldn't be done. It was ironic that in the freezing of ice and the making of glaciers the planet itself could store cold.

Also, there would be monstrous storms and blizzards on Lani II as cold conditions got worse. The wire-grids could be held aloft for shorter and shorter periods, and each time they would pull down less power than before. Their effectiveness would diminish even faster than the need for effectiveness increased.

Bordman felt even deeper depression as he worked out the facts. His proposal was essentially futile. It would be encouraging, and to a very slight degree and for a certain short time it would palliate the situation on the inner planet. But in the long run its effect would be zero.

He was embarrassed, too, that Herndon was so admiring. Herndon would tell Riki that he was marvelous. This trick of a flier-supported grid was not new. It had been used on Saril to supply power for giant peristaltic pumps emptying a polder that had been formed inside a ring of indifferently upraised islands.

*All I know,* thought Bordman bitterly, *is what somebody's showed me or I've read in books. And nobody's showed or written how to handle a thing like this!*

He went to Herndon's desk. Herndon had made a new graph of the solar-constant observations forwarded from home. It was a strictly typical curve of the results of coinciding cyclic change. It was the curve of a series of frequencies at the moment when they were all precisely in phase. From this much one could extrapolate and compute.

Bordman took a pencil, frowning. His fingers clumsily formed equations and solved them. The result was just about as bad as it could be. The change in brightness of the sun Lani would not be enough to be observed on Kent IV, the nearest other inhabited world, when light reached there four years from now. Lani would never be classed as a variable star, because the total change in light and heat would be relatively minute. The formula for computing planetary temperatures is not simple. Among its factors are squares and cubes of the variables. Worse, the heat radiated from a sun's photosphere varies not as the square or cube, but as the fourth power of its absolute temperature.

Bordman's computations were not pure theory. The data came from Sol itself, where alone in the galaxy there had been daily solar-constant measurements for three hundred years. The rest of his deductions were based ultimately on Earth observations, too. Most scientific data had to refer back to Earth to get an adequate continuity. And there could be no possible doubt about the sunspot data, because Sol and Lani were of the same type and nearly equal size.

Using the figures on the present situation, Bordman reluctantly arrived at the fact that here, on this already-frozen world, the temperature would drop gradually until $CO_2$ froze out of the atmosphere. When that happened, the temperature would plummet until there was no really significant difference between it and that of empty space. It is carbon dioxide which is responsible for the greenhouse effect, by which a planet is in thermal equilibrium only at a temperature above its surroundings, as a greenhouse in sunlight is warmer than the outside air.

The greenhouse effect would vanish soon on the colony world. When it vanished on the mother planet. . . .

Bordman found himself thinking, *if Riki won't leave when the Survey ship comes, I'll resign from the Service. I'll have to if I'm to stay. And I won't go unless she does.*

"If you want to come, it's all right," said Bordman ungraciously.

He waited while Riki slipped into the bulky cold-garments that were needed out-of-doors in the daylight, and were doubly necessary at night. There were heavy boots with inches-thick insulating soles, made in one piece with the many-layered trousers. There was an air-puffed, insulated over-tunic with its hood and mittens which were a part of the sleeves.

"Nobody goes outside at night," she said when they stood together in the cold-lock.

"I do," he told her. "I want to find out something."

The outer door opened and he stepped out. He held his arm for her, because the steps and walkway were no longer heated. Now they were covered with a filmy layer of powder — microscopic snow-crystals frozen out of the air by the unbearable chill of night.

There was no moon, of course, yet the ice-clad mountains glowed faintly. The drone-hulls arranged in such an orderly fashion were dark against the frosted ground. There was silence, stillness, the feeling of ancient quietude. No wind stirred anywhere. Nothing moved, nothing lived. The soundlessness was enough to crack the ear-drums.

Bordman threw back his head and gazed at the sky for a very long time. Nothing. He looked down at Riki.

"Look at the sky," he commanded.

She raised her eyes. She had been watching him. But as she gazed upward she almost cried out. The sky was filled with stars in innumerable variety. But the brighter ones were as stars had never been seen before. Just as the sun in daylight had been accompanied by sun-dogs — pale phantoms of itself ranged about it — so the brighter distant suns now shone from the center of rings of their own images. They no longer had the look of random placing. Those which were most distinct were patterns in themselves, and one's eye strove instinctively to grasp the greater pattern in which such seeming artifacts must belong.

"Oh — beautiful!" cried Riki softly.

"Look!" he insisted. "Keep looking."

She continued to gaze, moving her eyes about hopefully. It was such a sight as no one could have imagined. Every tint and every color, every possible degree of brightness appeared. And there were groups of stars of the same brilliance which almost made triangles, but not quite. There were rose-tinted stars which almost formed an arc, but did not. And there were arrays which were almost lines and nearly formed squares and polygons, but never actually achieved them.

"It's beautiful," said Riki. "But what must I look for?"

"Look for what isn't there," he ordered.

She looked, and the stars were unwinking, but that was not extraordinary. They filled all the firmament, without the least space in which some tiny sparkle of light was not to be found. But that was not remarkable, either. Then there was a vague flickering graying glow somewhere, indefinite. It vanished. Then she realized.

"There's no aurora!" she exclaimed.

"That's it," said Bordman. "There've always been auroras here. But no longer. We may be responsible. I wish I thought it wise to turn everything back to reservoir power for a while. We could find out. But we can't afford it."

"I looked at it when we first landed," admitted Riki. "It was unbelievable. But it was terribly cold, out of shelter. And it happened every night, so I said to myself I'd look tomorrow, and then tomorrow again. So it got so I never looked at all."

Bordman kept his eyes where that faint gray flickering had been. And, once one realized, it was astonishing that the former nightly play of ghostly color should be absent.

"The aurora," he said, "happens in the very upper limits of the air, fifty — seventy — ninety miles up, when God-knows-what emitted particles from the sun come streaking in, drawn by the planet's magnetic field. The aurora's a phenomenon of ions. We tap the ionosphere a long way down from where it plays, but I'm wondering if we stopped it."

"We?" said Riki, shocked. "We humans?"

"We tap the ions of their charges," he said somberly, "that the sunlight made by day. We're pulling in all the power we can. I wonder if we've drained the aurora of its energy, too."

Riki was silent. Bordman gazed, still searching. But he shook his head.

"It could be," he said in a carefully detached voice. "We didn't draw much power by comparison with the amount that came. But the ionization is an ultra-violet effect. Atmospheric gases don't ionize too easily. After all, if the solar constant dropped a very little, it might mean a terrific drop in the ultra-violet part of the spectrum — and that's what makes ions of oxygen and nitrogen and hydrogen and such. The ion-drop could easily be fifty times as great as the drop in the solar constant. And we're drawing power from the little that's left."

Riki stood very still. The cold was horrible. Had there been a wind, it could not have been endured for an instant. But the air was motionless. Yet its coldness was so great that the inside of one's nostrils ached, and the inside of one's chest was aware of chill. Even through the cold-garments there was the feeling as of ice without.

"I'm beginning," said Bordman, "to suspect that I'm a fool. Or maybe I'm an optimist. It might be the same thing. I could have guessed that the power we could draw would drop faster than our need for power increased. If we've drained the aurora of its light, we're scraping the bottom of the barrel. And it's a shallower barrel than one would suspect."

There was stillness again. Riki stood mousy-quiet. *When she realized what this means,* thought Bordman grimly, *she won't admire me so much. Her brother's built me up. But I've been a fool, figuring out excuses to hope. She'll see it.*

"I think," said Riki, "that you're telling me that after all we can't store up heat to live on, down in the mine."

"We can't," agreed Bordman. "Not much, nor long. Not enough to matter."

"So we won't live as long as Ken expects?"

"Not nearly as long," said Bordman. "He's hoping we can find out things to be useful back on Lani II. But we'll lose the power we can get from our grid long before even their new grids are useless. We'll have to start using our reserve power a lot sooner. It'll be gone — and us with it — before they're really in straits for living-heat."

Riki's teeth began to chatter.

"This sounds like I'm scared," she said angrily, "but I'm not! I'm just freezing. If you want to know, I'd a lot rather have it the way you say. I won't have to grieve over anybody, and they'll be too bust to grieve for me . . . Let's go inside while it's still warm."

He helped her back into the cold-lock, and the outer door closed. She was shivering uncontrollably when the warmth came pouring in.

They went into Herndon's office. He came in as Riki was peeling off the top part of her cold-garments. She still shivered. He glanced at her and said to Bordman:

"There's been a call from the grid-control shack. It looks like there's something wrong, but they can't find anything. The grid is set for maximum power-collection, but it's bringing in only fifty thousand kilowatts!"

"We're on our way back to savagery," said Bordman, with an

attempt at irony.

It was true. A man can produce two hundred fifty watts from his muscles for a reasonable length of time. When he had no more power, he is a savage. When he gains a kilowatt of energy from the muscles of a horse, he is a barbarian, but the new power cannot be directed wholly as he wills. When he can apply it to a plow he has high barbarian culture, and when he adds still more he begins to be civilized. Steam-power put as much as four kilowatts to work for every human being in the first industrialized countries, and in the mid-twentieth century there were sixty kilowatts per person in the more advanced nations. Nowadays, of course, a modern culture assumed five hundred as a minimum. But there was less than half that in the colony on Lani III. And its environment made its own demands.

"There can't be any more," said Riki, trying to control her shivering. "We're even using the aurora and there isn't any more power. It's running out. We'll go even before the people at home, Ken."

Herndon's features looked pinched.

"But we can't! We mustn't!" He turned to Bordman. "We do them good, back home! There was panic. Our report about cable grids has put heart in people. They're setting to work magnificently! So we're some use. They know we're worse off then they are, and as long as we hold on they'll be encouraged. We've got to keep going somehow!"

Riki breathed deeply until her shivering stopped. Then she said:

"Haven't you noticed, Ken, that Mr. Bordman has the viewpoint of his profession? His business is finding things wrong. He was deposited in our midst to detect defects in what we did and do. He has the habit of looking for the worst. But I think he can turn the habit to good use. He did turn up the idea of cable-grids."

"Which," said Bordman, "turns out to be no good at all. They'd be some good if they weren't needed, really. But the conditions that make them necessary make them useless!"

Riki shook her head.

"They are useful!" she said. "They're keeping people at home from despairing. Now, though, you've got to think of something else. If you think of enough things, one will do good the way you want, more than just making people feel better."

"What does it matter how people feel?" he demanded bitterly. "What difference do feelings make? One can't change facts!"

Riki said firmly:

"We humans are the only creatures in the universe who don't do anything else. Every other creature accepts facts. It lives where it is born, and it feeds on the food that is there for it, and it dies when the facts of nature require it to. We humans don't. Especially the women! We won't let men do it, either. When we don't like facts — mostly about ourselves — we change them. But important facts we disapprove of — we ask men to change them for us. And they do!"

She faced Bordman. Rather incredibly, she grinned at him.

"Will you please change the facts that look so annoying just now, please? Please?" Then she elaborately pantomimed an over-feminine girl's look of wide-eyed admiration. "You're so big and strong! I just know you can do it — for me!"

She abruptly dropped the pretense and moved toward the door. She half-turned then, and said detachedly:

"But about half of that is true."

The door slid shut behind her. It suddenly occurred to Bordman that she knew a Colonial Survey ship was due to stop by here to pick him up. She believed he expected to be rescued, even though the rest of the colony could not be, and most of it wouldn't consent to leave their kindred when the death of mankind in this solar system took place. He said awkwardly:

"Fifty thousand kilowatts isn't enough to land a ship."

Herndon frowned. Then he said:

"Oh. You mean the Survey ship that's to pick you up can't land? But it can go in orbit and put down a rocket landing-boat for you."

"I wasn't thinking of that. I'd something more in mind. I — rather like your sister. She's pretty wonderful. But there are some other women here in the colony, too. About a dozen all told. As a matter or self-respect I think we ought to get them away on the Survey ship. I agree that they wouldn't consent to go. But if they had no choice — if we could get them on board the grounded ship, and they suddenly found themselves — well — kidnapped and outward-bound not by their own fault . . . They could be faced with the accomplished fact that they had to go on living."

Herndon said evenly:

"That's been in the back of my mind for some time. Yes, I'm for that. But the Survey ship can't land —"

"I believe I can land it regardless," said Bordman. I can find out, anyhow. I'll need to try things. I'll need help. But I want your promise that if I can get the ship to ground you'll conspire with her skipper and arrange for them to go on living."

Herndon looked at him.

"Some new stuff, in a way," said Bordman uncomfortably. "I'll have to stay aground to work it. It's also part of the bargain that I shall. And of course your sister can't know about it, or she can't be fooled into living."

Herndon's expression changed a little.

"What'll you do? Of course it's a bargain."

"I'll need some metals we haven't smelted so far," said Bordman. "Potassium if I can get it, sodium if I can't, and at worst I'll settle for zinc. Cesium would be best, but we've found no traces of it."

Herndon said thoughtfully:

"No-o-o. I think I can get you sodium and potassium, from rocks. I'm afraid no zinc. How much?"

"Grams," said Bordman. "Trivial quantities. And I'll need a miniature landing-grid built. Very miniature."

Herndon shrugged his shoulders.

"It's over my head. But just to have work to do will be good for everybody. We've been feeling more frustrated here than any other humans in history. I'll go round up the men who'll do the work. You talk to them."

The door closed behind him. Bordman got out of his cold-clothing. He thought, *She'll rage when she finds her brother and I have deceived her.* Then he thought of the other women. *If any of them are married, we'll have to see if there's room for their husbands. I'll have to dress up the idea. Make it look like reason for hope, or the women would find out. But not many can go. . . .*

He knew roughly how many extra passengers could be carried on a Survey ship, even in such an emergency as this. Living-quarters were not luxurious, at best. Everything was cramped and skimped. Survey ships were rugged, tiny vessels, which performed their duties amid tedium and discomfort and peril for all on board. But one of them could carry away a very few unwilling refugees to Kent IV.

He settled down at Herndon's desk to work out the thing to be done.

It was not unreasonable. Tapping the ionosphere for power was something like pumping water out of a pipe-well in sand. If the water-table was high, there was pressure to force the water to the pipe, and one could pump fast. If the water-table was low, water couldn't flow fast enough. The pump would suck dry. In the ionosphere, the level of ionization was at once like the pressure and the size of the sand-grains. When the level was high, the flow was vast because the sand-grains were large and the conductivity high. But as the level lessened, so did the size of the sand-grains. There was less to draw, and more resistance to its flow.

However, there had been one tiny flicker of auroral light over by the horizon. There was still power aloft. If Bordman could in a fashion prime the pump, if he could increase the conductivity by increasing the ions present around the place where their charges were drawn away, he could increase the total flow. It would be like digging a brick well where a pipe well had been. A brick well draws water from all around its circumference.

So Bordman computed carefully. It was ironic that he had to go to such trouble simply because he didn't have test-rockets like the Survey uses to get a picture of a planet's weather-pattern. They rise vertically for fifty miles or so, trailing a thread of sodium vapor behind them. The trail is detectable for some time, and ground instruments record each displacement by winds blowing in different directions at different speeds, one over the other. Such a rocket with its loading slightly changed would do all Bordman had in mind. But he didn't have one, so something much more elaborate was called for.

A landing-grid has to be not less than half a mile across and two thousand feet high because its field has to reach out five planetary diameters to handle ships that land and take off. To handle solid objects it has to be accurate, though power can be drawn with an improvisation. To thrust a sodium vapor bomb anywhere from twenty to fifty miles high, he'd need a grid over six feet wide and five high. It could throw much higher, of course, and hold what it threw. But doubling the size would make accuracy easier.

He tripled the dimensions. There would be a grid eighteen feet across and fifteen high. Tuned to the casing of a small bomb, it could hold it steady at seven hundred fifty thousand feet, far beyond necessity. He began to make the detail drawings.

Herndon came back with half a dozen chosen colonists. They were young men, technicians rather than scientists. Some of them were several years younger than Bordman. There were grim and stunned expressions on some faces, but one tried to pretend nonchalance, and two seemed trying to suppress fury at the monstrous occurrence that would destroy not only their own lives, but everything they remembered on the planet which was their home. They looked almost challengingly at Bordman.

He explained. He was going to put a cloud of metallic vapor up in the ionosphere. Sodium if he had to, potassium if he could, zinc if he must. Those metals were readily ionized by sunlight, much more readily than atmospheric gases. In effect, he was going to supply a certain area of the ionosphere with material to increase the efficiency of sunshine in providing electric power. As a sideline, there would be increased conductivity from the normal ionosphere.

"Something like this was done centuries ago, back on Earth," he explained. "They used rockets, and made sodium-vapor clouds as much as twenty and thirty miles long. Even nowadays the Survey uses test rockets with trails of sodium vapor. It will work to some degree. We'll find out how much."

He felt Herndon's eyes upon him. They were almost dazedly respectful. But one of the technicians said:

"How long will those clouds last?"

"That high, three or four days," Bordman told him. "They won't help much at night, but they should step up power-intake while the sun shines on them."

A man in the back said, "Hup!" The significance was, "Let's go!"

Somebody else said feverishly, "What do we do? Got working drawings? Who makes the bombs? Who does what? Let's get at this!"

Then there was confusion, and Herndon vanished. Bordman suspected he'd gone to have Riki put this theory into dot-and-dash code for beam-transmission back to Lani II. But there was no time to stop him. These men wanted precise information and it was half an hour before the last of them had gone out with free-hand sketches, and had come back for further explanation of a doubtful point, and other men had come in to demand a share in the job.

When he was alone again, Bordman thought, *Maybe it's worth doing because it'll get Riki on the Survey ship. But they think it means saving the people back home!*

Which it didn't. Taking energy out of sunlight is taking energy out of sunlight, no matter how you do it. Take it out as electric power, and there's less heat left. Warm one place with electric power and everywhere else is a little colder. There's an equation. On this colony-world it wouldn't matter, but on the home world it would. The more there was trickery to gather heat, the more heat would be needed. . . . Again it might postpone the death of twenty million people, but it would never, never prevent it. . . .

The door slid aside and Riki came in. She stammered a little.

"I just coded what Ken told me to send back home. It will — it will do everything! It's wonderful! I wanted to tell you!"

"Consider," Bordman said, in a desperate attempt to take it lightly, "that I've taken a bow."

He tried to smile. It was not a success. And Riki suddenly drew a deep breath and looked at him in a new fashion.

"Ken's right," she said softly. "He says you can't get conceited. You're not satisfied with yourself even now, are you?" She smiled. "But what I like is that you aren't really smart. A woman can make you do things. I have!"

He looked at her uneasily. She grinned.

"I, even I, can at least pretend to myself that I helped bring this about! If I hadn't said please change the facts that are so annoying, and if I hadn't said you were big and strong and clever. . . . I'm going to tell myself for the rest of my life that I helped make you do it!"

Bordman swallowed.

"I'm afraid," he said, "that it won't work again."

She cocked her head on one side.

"No?"

He stared at her apprehensively. And then with a bewildering change of emotional reaction, he saw that her eyes were filled with tears. She stamped her foot.

"You're horrible!" she cried. "Here I came in, and — and if you think you can get me kidnapped to safety without even telling me that you 'rather like' me, as you told my brother, or that I'm 'pretty wonderful —'"

He was stunned, that she knew. She stamped her foot again.

"For Heaven's sake!" she wailed. "Do I have to *ask* you to kiss me?"

During the last night of preparation, Bordman sat by a thermometer registering the outside temperature. He hovered over it as one might over a sick child. He watched it and sweated, though the inside temperature of the drone-hull was lowered to save power. There was nothing he could actually do. At midnight the thermometer said it was seventy degrees below zero Fahrenheit. The hour before dawn it was eighty-five degrees below zero. Then he sweated profusely. The meaning of the slowed descent was that carbon dioxide was being frozen out of the upper layers of the atmosphere. The frozen particles were drifting slowly downward, and as they reached lower and faintly warmer levels they returned to the state of gas. But there was a level, above the $CO_2$, where the temperature was plummeting.

The height to which carbon dioxide existed was dropping. Slowly, but inexorably. And above the carbon-dioxide level there was no bottom limit to the temperature. The greenhouse effect was due to $CO_2$. Where it wasn't, the cold of space moved down. If at ground-level the thermometer read ever-so-slightly less than one hundred nine below zero, then everything was finished. Without the greenhouse effect, the night-side of the planet would lose its remaining heat with a rush. Even the day side, once cold enough, would lose heat to emptiness as fast as it came from the sun. If it went down to that it would plunge to a hundred and fifty or two hundred degrees below zero, or more. And it would never come up again.

There would be rain at nightfall, a rain of oxygen frozen to a liquid and splashing on the ground. Human life would be impossible, in any shelter and under any conditions. Even spacesuits would not protect against an atmosphere sucking heat from it at that rate. A spacesuit can be heated against the loss of temperature due to radiation in a vacuum. It could not be heated against nitrogen which would chill it, irresistibly by contact.

But, as Bordman sweated over it, the thermometer steadied at minus eighty-five degrees. When the dawn came, it rose to seventy. By mid-morning, the temperature in bright sunlight was no lower than sixty-five below zero.

But there was no bounce left in Bordman when Herndon came for him.

"Your phone-plate's been flashing," said Herndon, "and you didn't answer. Must have had your back to it. Riki's over in the mine, watching them get things ready. She was worried that she couldn't call you. Asked me to find out what was the trouble."

"Has she got something to heat the air she breathes?" asked Bordman.

"Naturally," said Herndon. He added curiously, "What's the matter?"

"We almost took our licking," Bordman told him. "I'm afraid for tonight, and tomorrow night too. If the $CO_2$ freezes —"

"We'll have power!" Herndon insisted. "We'll build ice-tunnels and ice-domes. We'll build a city under ice, if we have to. But we'll have power!"

"I doubt it very much," said Bordman. "I wish you hadn't told Riki of the bargain to get her away from here when the Survey ship comes!"

Herndon grinned.

"Is the little grid ready?" asked Bordman.

"Everything's set," said Herndon. "It's in the mine-tunnel with radiant heaters playing on it. The bombs are ready. We made enough to last for months, while we were at it. No use taking chances!"

Bordman looked at him queerly. Then he said:

"We might as well go out and try the thing, then."

He put on the cold-garments as they were now modified for the increased frigidity. Nobody could breathe air at minus sixty-five degrees without getting his lungs frost-bitten. So there was now a plastic mask to cover one's face, and the air one breathed outdoors was heated as it came through a wire-gauze snout. But still it was not wise to stay out of shelter for too long a time.

Bordman and Herndon went out-of-doors. They stepped out of the cold-lock and gazed about them. The sun seemed markedly paler and now it had lost its sun-dogs again. Ice-crystals no longer floated in the almost congealed air. The sky was dark. It was almost purple, and it seemed to Bordman that he could detect faint flecks of light in it. They would be stars, shining in the day-time.

There seemed no one about at all, only the white coldness of the mountains. But there was a movement at the mine-drift, and something came out of it. Four men appeared, muffled up like Bordman himself. They rolled the eighteen-foot grid out of the mine-mouth, moving it on those inflated bags which are so much better than rollers for rough terrain. They looked absurdly like bears with steaming noses in their masks and clothing. They had some sort of powered pusher with them and they got the metal cage to the very top of a rounded stone upcrop which rose in the center of the valley.

"We picked that spot," said Herndon's muffled voice through the chill, "because by shifting the grid's position it can be aimed, and be on a solid base. Right?"

"Quite all right," said Bordman. "We'll go work it."

The two men walked across the valley, in which nothing moved except the padded figures of the four technicians. Their wire-gauze breathing-masks seemed to emit smoke. They waved to Bordman in greeting.

*I'm popular again*, he thought drearily, *but it doesn't matter. Getting the Survey ship to ground won't help now, since Riki's fore-warned. And this trick won't solve anything permanently on the home planet. It'll just postpone things.*

Even when Riki, muffled like the rest, waved to him from the mouth of the tunnel, his spirits did not lift. The thing he wanted was to look forward to years and years of being with Riki. He wanted, in fact, to look forward to forever. And there might not be a tomorrow.

"I had the control-board rolled out here," she called through her mask. "It's cold, but you can watch!"

It wouldn't be much to watch. If everything went all right, some dial-needles would kick over violently and their readings would go up and up. But they wouldn't be readings of temperature. Presently the big grid would report increased power from the sky. But tonight the temperature would drop a little farther. Tomorrow night it would drop further still. When it reached one hundred nine point three degrees below zero at ground-level, that would be the finish.

Another of the figures that looked like a bear now went out of the mine-mouth, trudging toward the grid. It carried a muffled, well-wrapped object in its arms. It stopped and crept between the spokes of the grid, and put the object on the stone. Bordman traced cables with his eyes, from the grid to the control-board, and from the board back to the reserve-power storage cells, deep in the mountain.

"The grid's tuned to the bomb," said Riki, close beside him. "I checked that myself!"

The bear-like figure out in the valley jerked at the bomb. There was a small rising cloud of grayish vapor. It continued. The figure climbed hastily out of the grid. When the man was clear, Bordman threw a switch.

There was a thin whining sound, and the wrapped, smoking object leaped upward. It seemed to fall toward the sky. There was no more of drama than that. An object the size of a basketball fell upward, swiftly, until it disappeared.

Bordman sat quite still, watching the control-board dials. Presently he corrected this, and shifted that. He did not want the bomb to have too high an upward velocity. At a hundred thousand feet it would find very little air to stop the rise of the vapor it was to release.

The field-focus dial reached its indication of one hundred thousand feet. Bordman reversed the lift-switch. He counted, and then switched the power off. The small, thin whine ended.

He threw the power-intake switch. The power-yield needle stirred.

The minute grid was drawing power like its vaster counterpart, but its field was infinitesimal by comparison. It drew power as a soda-straw might draw water from wet sand.

Then the intake-needle kicked. It swung sharply, and wavered, and then began a steady, even, climbing movement across the markings of the dial-face. Riki was not watching that.

"They see something!" she panted. "Look at them!"

The four men who had trundled the smaller grid to its place, now stared upward. They flung out their arms. One of them jumped up and down. They leaped. They practically danced.

"Let's go see," said Bordman.

He went out of the tunnel with Riki. They gazed upward. And directly overhead, where the sky was darkest blue and where it had seemed that stars shone through the daylight, there was a minute cloud. But it grew. Its edges were yellow, saffron-yellow. It expanded and spread. Presently it began to thin. As it thinned, it began to shine. It was luminous. And the luminosity had a strange, familiar quality.

Somebody came panting down the tunnel, from inside the mountain.

"The grid —" he panted. "The big grid! It's pumping power! Big power! BIG power!"

But Bordman was looking at the sky, as if he did not quite believe his eyes. The cloud now expanded very slowly, but still it grew. And it was not regular in shape. The bomb had not shattered quite evenly, and the vapor had poured out more on one side than the other. There was a narrow, arching arm of brightness. . . . "It looks," said Riki breathlessly, "like a comet!"

And then Bordman froze in every muscle. He stared at the cloud he had made aloft, and his hands clenched in their mittens, and he swallowed behind his cold-mask.

"Th-that's it," he said in a hushed voice. "It's — *very* much like a comet. I'm glad you said that! We cane make something even more like a comet. We can use all the bombs we've made, right away, to make it. And we've got to hurry so it won't get any colder tonight!"

Which, of course, sounded like insanity. Riki looked apprehensively at him. But Bordman had just thought of something. And nobody had taught it to him and he hadn't gotten it out of books. But he'd seen a comet.

The new idea was so promising that he regarded it with anguished unease for fear it would not hold up. It was an idea that really ought to change the facts resulting naturally from a lowered solar constant in a sol-type star.

Half the colony set to work to make more bombs when the effect of the first bomb showed up. The men were not very efficient at first, because they tended to want to stop work and dance from time to time. But they worked with an impassioned enthusiasm. They made more bomb-casings, and they prepared more sodium and potassium metal and more fuses, and more insulation to wrap around the bombs to protect them from the cold of airless space.

Because these were to go out to airlessness. The miniature grid could lift and hold a bomb steady in its field-focus at seven hundred and fifty thousand feet. But if a bomb was accelerated all the way out to that point, and the field was then snapped off. . . . Why, it wasn't held anywhere! It kept on going with its attained velocity. And it burst when its fuse decided that it should, whereupon immediately a mass of sodium and potassium vapor, mixed with the fumes of high explosive, flung itself madly in all directions, out between the stars. Absolute vacuum tore the compressed gasified metals apart. The separate atoms, white-hot from the explosion, went swirling through sunlit space. The sunlight was dimmed a trifle, to be sure. But individual atoms of the lighter alkaline-earth metals have marked photoelectric properties. In sunshine these gas-molecules ionized, and therefore spread more widely, and did not coalesce into even microscopic droplets.

They formed, in fact, a cloud in space. An ionized cloud, in which no particle was too large to be responsive to the pressure of light. The cloud acted like the gases of a comet's tail. It was a comet's tail, though there was no comet. And it was an extraordinary comet's tail because it is said that you can put a comet's tail in your hat, at normal atmospheric pressure. But this could not have been put in a hat. Even before it turned to gas, it was the size of a basketball. And, in space, it glowed.

It glowed with the brightness of the sunshine on it, which was light that would normally have gone away through the interstellar dark. And it filled one corner of the sky. Within one hour it was a comet tail ten thousand miles long, which visibly brightened the daytime heavens. And it was only the first such reflecting clouds.

The next bomb set for space exploded in a different quarter, because Bordman had had the miniature grid wrestled around the upcrop to point in a new and somewhat more carefully chosen line. The next spattered brilliance in a different section still. And the brilliance lasted.

Bordman flung his first bombs recklessly, because there would be more, and because he was desperately anxious to hang as many comet-tails as possible around the colony-planet before nightfall. He didn't want it to get any colder.

And it didn't. In fact, there wasn't exactly any real nightfall on Lani III that night.

The planet turned on its axis, to be sure. But around it, quite close by, there hung gigantic streamers of shining gas. At their beginning, those streamer bore a certain resemblance to the furry wild-animal tails that little boys like to have hanging down from hunting-caps. Only they shone. And as they developed they merged, so that there was an enormous shining curtain about Lani III, draperies of metal-dust to capture sunlight that would otherwise have been wasted, and to diffuse much of it on Lani II. At midnight three was only one spot in all the night sky where there was really darkness. That was overhead, directly outward from the planet, opposite the sun. Gigantic shining streamers formed a wall, a tube, of comet-tail material, yet many times more dense and therefore more bright, which shielded the colony world against the dark and cold, and threw upon it a shining, warming brightness.

Riki maintained stoutly that she could feel the warmth from the sky, but that was improbable. However, heat certainly did come from somewhere. The thermometer did not fall at all, that night. It rose. It was up to fifty below zero at dawn. During the day — they sent out twenty more bombs that second day — it was up to twenty degrees below zero. By the day after, there were completed computations from the home planet, and the concrete results of abstruse speculation, and the third day's bombs were placed with optimum spacing for heating purposes.

But dawn of the fourth day the air was a balmy five degrees below zero, and the day after that there was a small running stream in the valley at midday.

There was talk of stocking the stream with fish, on the morning the Survey ship came in. The great landing-grid gave out a deep-toned, vibrant, humming note, like the deepest possible note of the biggest organ that could be imagined. A speck appeared high up in a pale-blue sky with trimmings of golden gas clouds. The Survey ship came down and down and settled as a shining silver object in the very center of the gigantic red-painted landing-grid.

Her skipper came to find Bordman. He was in Herndon's office. The skipper struggled to keep sheer blankness out of his expression.

"What the hell?" he demanded. "This is the damndest sight in the whole Galaxy, and they tell me you're responsible! There've been ringed planets, before, and there've been comets and who knows what! But shining gas-pipes aimed at the sun, half a million miles across! And there are two of them — both the occupied planets!"

Herndon explained why the curtains hung in space. There was a drop in the solar constant. . . .

The skipper exploded. He wanted facts! Details! Something to report!

Bordman was automatically on the defensive when the skipper swung his questions at him. A Senior Colonial Survey officer is not revered by the Survey ship-service officers. Men like Bordman can be a nuisance to a hard-working ship's officer. They have to be carried to unlikely places for their work of checking over colonial installations. They have to be put down on hard-to-get-at colonies, and they have to be called for, sometimes, at times and places which are inconvenient. So a man in Bordman's position is likely to feel unpopular.

"I'd just finished the survey here," he said defensively, "when a cycle of sunspot cycles matured. All the sunspot periods got in phase, and the solar constant dropped. So I naturally offered what help I could to meet the situation."

The skipper regarded him incredulously.

"But it couldn't be done!" he said. "They told me how you did it, but it couldn't be done! Do you realize that these vapor curtains will make fifty borderline worlds fit for use? Half a pound of sodium a week!" He gestured helplessly. "They tell me the amount of heat reaching the surface here has been upped by fifteen percent! D'you realize what *that* means?"

"I haven't been worrying about it," admitted Bordman. "There was a local situation and something had to be done. I — er — remembered things, and Riki suggested something I mightn't have thought of. So it's worked out like this." Then he said abruptly: "I'm not leaving. I'll let you take my resignation back. I think I'm going to settle here. It'll be a long time before we get really temperate-climate conditions here, but we can warm up a valley like this for cultivation, and it's going to be a rather satisfying job. It's a brand new planet with a brand new ecological system to be established."

The skipper of the Survey ship sat down hard. Then the sliding door of Herndon's office opened and Riki came in. The skipper stood up again. Bordman awkwardly made the introduction. Riki smiled.

"I'm telling him," said Bordman, "that I'm resigning from the Service to settle down here."

Riki nodded. She put her hand in proprietary fashion on Bordman's arm. The Survey skipper cleared his throat.

"I'm not going to carry your resignation," he said. "There've got to be detailed reports on how this business works. Dammit, if vapor clouds in space can be used to keep a planet warm, they can be used to shade a planet, too! If you resign, somebody else will have to come out here and make observations and work out the details of the trick. Nobody could be gotten here in less than a year! You've got to stay here to build up a report, and you ought to be available for consultation when this thing's to be done somewhere else. I'll report that I insisted as a Survey emergency —"

Riki said confidently:

"Oh, that's all right! He'll do it! Of course! Won't you?"

Bordman nodded. He thought, *I've been lonely all my life. I've never belonged anywhere. But nobody could possibly belong anywhere as thoroughly as I'll belong here when it's warm and green and even the grass on the ground is partly my doing. But Riki'll like for me still to be in the Service. Women like to see their husbands wearing uniforms.*

And he said:

"Of course. If it really needs to be done. Though you realize that there's nothing really remarkable about it. Everything I've done has been what I was taught, or read in books."

"Hush!" said Riki. "You're wonderful!"

And so they were married, and Bordman was very, very happy. But people who can serve their fellow-men are never left alone. We humans get into so many predicaments!

Bordman had lived contentedly on Lani III for only three years when there was an emergency on Kalen IV and no other qualified Space Survey officer could possibly be gotten to the spot in time to handle it. A special ship raced to ask him to act — just for this once. And, reluctantly, he went to do what he could, with the assurance to Riki that he would be back in three months. But he was gone for two years, and his youngest child did not remember him when he came back.

He stayed home one year, and then there was an emergency on Seth IV. That kept him only four months, but before he could get back to Lani he was urgently required to check out a colony on Aleph I, whose colonists could not enter into possession until a short-handed Survey service licensed it. Then there was another call. . . .

In the first ten years of his marriage, Bordman spent less than five with his family. But he didn't like it. When he'd been married fifteen years he'd made it clear at Headquarters that he was only carrying on until a new class graduated from Space Survey training. Then he was going home to stay.

# II

## SAND DOOM

Bordman knew there was something wrong when the throbbing, acutely uncomfortable vibration of rocket-blasts shook the ship. Rockets were strictly emergency devices, these days, so when they were used there was obviously an emergency.

He sat still. He had been reading in the passenger-lounge of the *Warlock* — a very small lounge indeed — but as a Senior Colonial Survey Officer with considerable experience he was well-traveled enough to know when things did not go right. He looked up from the book-screen, waiting. Nobody came to explain the eccentricity of a spaceship using rockets. The explanation would have been immediate on a regular liner, but the *Warlock* was practically a tramp. This trip it carried just two passengers. Passenger service was not yet authorized to the planet, and would not be until Bordman had made the report he was on his way to compile. At the moment, though, the rockets blasted, and stopped, and blasted again. There was something definitely wrong.

The *Warlock's* other passenger came out of her cabin. She looked surprised. She was Aletha Redfeather, a very lovely Amerind. It was extraordinary that a girl could be so self-sufficient on a tedious space-voyage, and Bordman approved of her. She was making the journey to Xosa II as a representative of the Amerind Historical Society, but she'd brought her own book-reels and some elaborate fancy-work which — woman-fashion — she used to occupy her hands. She hadn't been at all a nuisance. Now she tilted her head on one side as she looked inquiringly at Bordman.

"I'm wondering, too," he told her, just as an especially sustained and violent shuddering of rocket-impulsion made his chair legs thutter on the floor.

There was a long period of stillness. Then another violent but much shorter blast. A shorter one still. Presently there was a half-second blast which must have been from a single rocket-tube because of the mild shaking it produced. After that there was nothing at all.

Bordman frowned to himself. He'd been anticipating ground-fall within a matter of hours, certainly. He'd just gone through his spec-book carefully and re-familiarized himself with the work he was to survey on Xosa II. It was a perfectly commonplace mineral-planet development, and he'd expected to clear it FE — fully established — and probably TP and NQ ratings as well, indicating that tourists were permitted and no quarantine was necessary. Considering the aridity of the planet, no bacteriological dangers could be expected to exist, and if tourists wanted to view its monstrous deserts and inferno-like wind-sculptures, they should be welcome.

But the ship had used rocket-drive in the planet's near vicinity. Emergency. Which was ridiculous. This was a pretty routine sort of voyage. Its purpose was the delivery of heavy equipment — specifically a smelter — and a Senior Colonial Survey Officer to report the completion of primary development.

Aletha waited, as if for more rocket-blasts. Presently she smiled at some thought that had occurred to her.

"If this were an adventure tape," she said, "the loudspeaker would now announce that the ship had established itself in an orbit around the strange, uncharted planet first sighted three days ago, and that volunteers were wanted for a boat landing."

Bordman demanded impatiently:

"Do you bother with adventure tapes? They're nonsense! A pure waste of time!"

Aletha smiled again.

"My ancestors," she told him, "used to hold tribal dances and make medicine and boast about how many scalps they'd taken and how they did it. It was satisfying — and educational for the young. Adolescents became familiar with the idea of what we nowadays call adventure. They were partly ready for it when it came. I suspect your ancestors used to tell each other stories about hunting mammoths and such. So I think it would be fun to hear that we were in orbit and that a boat landing was in order."

Bordman grunted. There were no longer adventures. The universe was settled, civilized. Of course there were still frontier planets — Xosa II was one — but pioneers had only hardships. Not adventures.

The ship-phone speaker clicked. It said curtly:

"*Notice. We have arrived at Xosa II and have established an orbit around it. Landing will be made by boat.*"

Bordman's mouth dropped open.

"What the devil's this?" he demanded.

"Adventure, maybe," said Aletha. Her eyes crinkled very pleasantly when she smiled. She wore a modern Amerind dress — a sign of pride in the ancestry which now implied such divers occupations as interstellar steel construction and animal husbandry and llano-planet colonization. "If it were adventure, as the only girl on the ship I'd have to be in the landing party, lest the tedium of orbital waiting make the —" her smile widened to a grin — "the pent-up restlessness of trouble-makers in the crew —"

The ship phone clicked again.

*"Mr. Bordman. Miss Redfeather. According to advices from the ground, the ship may have to stay in orbit for a considerable time. You will accordingly be landed by boat. Will you make yourselves ready, please, and report to the boat-blister?"* The voice paused and added. *"Hand luggage only, please."*

Aletha's eyes brightened. Bordman felt the shocked incredulity of a man accustomed to routine when routine is broken. Of course, survey ships made boat landings from orbit, and colony ships let down robot hulls by rocket when there was as yet no landing-grid for the handling of a ship. But never before in his experience had an ordinary freighter, on a routine voyage to a colony ready for a degree-of-completion survey, ever landed anybody by boat.

"This is ridiculous!" said Bordman, fuming.

"Maybe it's adventure," said Aletha. "I'll pack."

She disappeared into her cabin. Bordman hesitated. Then he went into his own. The colony on Xosa II had been established within six months. A temporary landing-grid for light supply ships was up within a year. It had permitted stockpiling, and it had been taken down to be rebuilt as a permanent grid with every possible contingency provided for. The eight months since the last ship landing was more than enough for the rebuilding of the gigantic, spidery, half-mile-high structure which would handle this planet's interstellar commerce. There was no excuse for an emergency. A boat landing was nonsensical!

He surveyed the contents of his cabin. Most of the cargo of the *Warlock* was smelter equipment which was to complete the outfitting of the colony. It was to be unloaded first. By the time the ship's holds were wholly empty, the smelter would be operating. The ship would wait for a full cargo of pig metal. Bordman had expected to live in this cabin while he worked on the survey he'd come to make and to leave again with the ship.

Now he was to go aground by boat. He fretted. The only emergency equipment he could possibly need was a heat-suit. He doubted the urgency of that. But he packed some clothing for indoors, and then defiantly included his spec-book and the volumes of definitive data to which specifications for structures and colonial establishments always referred. He'd get to work on his report immediately he landed.

He went out of the passengers' lounge to the boat-blister. An engineer's legs projected from the boat port. The engineer withdrew, with a strip of tape from the boat's computer. He compared it with a similar strip from the ship's figure box. Bordman consciously acted according to the best traditions of passengers.

"What's the trouble?" he asked.

"We can't land," said the engineer shortly.

He went away — according to the tradition by which ships' crews are always scornful of passengers.

Bordman scowled. Then Aletha came, carrying a not-too-heavy bag. Bordman put it in the boat, disapproving of the crampedness of the craft. But this wasn't a lifeboat. It was a landing-boat. A lifeboat had Lawlor drive and could travel light-years, but in the place of rockets and rocket fuel it had air purifiers and water recovery units and food stores. It couldn't land without a landing-grid aground, but it could get to a civilized planet. This landing boat could land without a grid, but its air wouldn't last long.

"Whatever's the matter," said Bordman darkly, "it's incompetence somewhere!"

But he couldn't figure it out. This was a cargo-ship. Cargo-ships neither took off nor landed under their own power. It was too costly of fuel they would have to carry. So landing-grids used local power — which did not have to be lifted — to heave ships out into space, and again used local power to draw them to ground again. Therefore ships carried fuel only for actual space flight, which was economy. Yet landing-grids had no moving parts to break down and no possibility of the failure of a power-source: landing-grids couldn't fail! So there couldn't be an emergency to make a ship ride orbit around a planet which had a landing-grid.

The engineer came back. He carried a mail sack full of letter-reels. He waved his hand. Aletha crawled into the landing boat port. Bordman followed. Four people, with considerable crowding, could have gotten into the little ship. Three pretty well filled it. The engineer followed them and sealed the port.

"Sealed off," he said into the microphone before him.

The exterior-pressure needle moved halfway across the dial. The interior-pressure needle stayed steady.

"All tight," said the engineer.

The exterior-pressure needle flicked to zero. There were clanking sounds. The long halves of the boat-blister stirred and opened, and abruptly the landing boat was in an elongated cup in the hull plating, and above them there were many, many stars. The enormous disk of a nearby planet floated into view around the hull. It was monstrous and blindingly bright. It was of a tawny color, with great, irregular areas of yellow and patches of bluishness. But most of it was the color of sand. And all its colors varied in shade — some placed lighter and some darker — and over at one edge there was blinding whiteness which could not be anything but an ice cap. Bordman knew that there was no ocean or sea or lake on all this whole planet, and the ice-cap was more nearly hoar-frost than such mile-deep glaciation as would be found at the poles of a maximum-comfort world.

"Strap in," said the engineer over his shoulder. "No-gravity coming, and then rocket-push. Settle your heads."

Bordman irritably strapped himself in. He saw Aletha busy at the same task, her eyes shining. Without warning, there came a sensation of acute discomfort. It was the landing boat, detaching itself from the ship and the diminishment of the ship's closely-confined artificial gravity field. That field suddenly dropped to nothingness, and Bordman had the momentary sickish dizziness that flicked-off gravity always produced. At the same time his heart pounded unbearably in this instinctive, racial-memory re-action to the feel of falling.

Then roaring. He was thrust savagely back against his seat. His tongue tried to slide back into his throat. There was an enormous oppression on his chest and he found himself thinking panicky profanity.

Simultaneously the vision ports went black, because they were out of the shadow of the ship. The landing boat turned — but there was no sensation of centrifugal force — and they were in a vast obscurity with merely a dim phantom of the planetary surface to be seen. Behind them a blue-white sun shone terribly. Its light was warm — hot — even though it came through the polarized, shielding ports.

"Did you say," panted Aletha happily — breathless because of the acceleration — "that there weren't any adventures?"

Bordman did not answer. But he did not count discomfort as an adventure.

The engineer did not look out the ports at all. He watched the screen before him. There was a vertical line across the side of the lighted ship. A blip moved downward across it, showing their height in thousands of miles. After a long time the blip reached the bottom, and the vertical line became double and another blip began to descend. It measured height in hundreds of miles. A bright spot — a square — appeared at one side of the screen. A voice muttered metallically, and suddenly seemed to shout, and then muttered again. Bordman looked out one of the black ports and saw the planet as if through smoked glass. It was a ghostly reddish thing which filled half the cosmos. It had mottlings, and its edge was curved. That would be the horizon.

The engineer moved controls and the white square moved. It went across the screen. He moved more controls. It came back to the center. The height-in-hundreds blip was at the bottom, now, and the vertical line tripled and a tens-of-miles-height blip crawled downward.

There were sudden, monstrous plungings of the landing boat. It had hit the outermost fringes of atmosphere. The engineer said words it was not appropriate for Aletha to hear. The plungings became more violent. Bordman held on, to keep from being shaken to pieces despite the straps, and stared at the murky surface of the planet. It seemed to be fleeing from them and they to be trying to overtake it. Gradually, very gradually, its flight appeared to slow. They were down to twenty miles, then.

Quite abruptly the landing boat steadied. The square spot bobbled about in the center of the astrogation-screen. The engineer worked controls to steady it.

The ports cleared a little. Bordman could see the ground below more distinctly. There were patches of every tint that mineral coloring could produce, and vast stretches of tawny sand. A little while more, and he could see the shadows of mountains. He made out mountain-flanks which should have had valleys between them and other mountain-flanks beyond, but they were joined by tawny flatness instead. These, he knew, would be the sand-plateaus which had been observed on this planet and which had only a still-disputed explanation. But he could see areas of glistening yellow and dirty white, and splashes of pink and streaks of ultramarine and gray and violet, and the incredible red of iron oxide covering square miles — too much to be believed.

The landing boat's rockets cut off. It coasted. Presently the horizon tilted and all the dazzling ground below turned sedately beneath them. Then came staccato instructions from a voice-speaker, which the engineer obeyed. The landing boat swung low — below the tips of giant mauve mountains with a sand-plateau beyond them — and its nose went up. It stalled.

Then the rockets roared again — and now, with air about them, they were horribly loud — and the boat settled down and down upon its own tail of fire.

A blinding mass of dust and rocket-fumes cut off all sight of everything else. Then a crunching crash, and the engineer swore peevishly to himself. He cut the rockets again. Finally.

Bordman found himself staring straight up, still strapped in his chair. The boat had settled on its own tail fins, and his feet were higher than his head. He felt ridiculous. He saw the engineer at work unstrapping himself, and duplicated the action, but it was absurdly difficult to get out of the chair.

Aletha managed more gracefully. She didn't need help.

"Wait," said the engineer ungraciously, "till somebody comes."

So they waited, using what had been chair-backs for seats.

The engineer moved a control and the windows cleared further. They saw the surface of Xosa II. There was no living thing in sight. The ground itself was pebbles and small rocks and minor boulders — all apparently tumbled from the starkly magnificent cliffs and mesas, every one eaten at in the unmistakable fashion of wind erosion. Through a notch in the mountain wall before them a strange, fan-shaped, frozen formation appeared. If such a thing had been credible, Bordman would have said that it was a flow of sand simulating a waterfall. And everywhere was a blinding brightness and the look and feel of blistering sunshine. But there was not one single leaf or twig or blade of grass. This was pure desert. This was Xosa II.

Aletha regarded it with bright eyes.

"Beautiful!" she said happily. "Isn't it?"

"Personally," said Bordman, "I never saw a place that looked less homelike or attractive."

Aletha laughed.

"My eyes see it differently."

Which was true. It was accepted, nowadays, that humankind might be one species but was many races, and each saw the cosmos in its own fashion. On Kalmet III there was a dense predominantly Asiatic population which terraced its mountainsides for agriculture and deftly mingled modern techniques with social customs not to be found on — say — Demeter I, where there were many red tiled stucco towns and very many olive groves. In the llano planets of the Equis cluster, Amerinds — Althea's kin — rode over plains dotted with the descendants of buffalo and antelope and cattle brought from ancient Earth. On the oases of Rustam IV there were date palms and riding camels and much argument about what should be substituted for the direction of Mecca at the times for prayer, while wheat-fields spanned provinces on Canna I and highly civilized emigrants from the continent of Africa on Earth stored jungle-gums and lustrous gems in the warehouses of their space-port city of Timbuk.

So it was natural for Aletha to look at this wind-carved wilderness otherwise than as Bordman did. Her racial kin were the pioneers of the stars, these days. Their heritage made them less than appreciative of urban life. Their inborn indifference to heights made them the steel construction men of the cosmos, and more than two thirds of the landing-beam grids in the whole galaxy had their coup-feather symbol on the key posts. But the planet government on Algonka V was housed in a three-thousand-foot stone teepee, and the best horses known to men were raised by ranchers with bronze skin and high cheekbones on the llano planet Chagan.

Now, here, in the *Warlock's* landing boat, the engineer snorted. A vehicle came around a cliff wall, clanking its way on those eccentric caterwheels that new-founded colonies find so useful. The vehicle glittered. It crawled over tumbled boulders, and flowed over fallen scree. It came briskly toward them.

"That's my cousin Ralph!" said Aletha in pleased surprise.

Bordman blinked and looked again. He did not quite believe his eyes. But they told the truth. The figure controlling the ground car was Indian — Amerind — wearing a breechcloth and thick-soled sandals and three streamlined feathers in a band about his head. Moreover, he did not ride the seat. He sat astride a semi-cylindrical part of the ground car, over which a gaily colored blanket had been thrown.

The ship's engineer rumbled disgustedly. But then Bordman saw how sane this method of riding was — here. The ground vehicle lurched and swayed and rolled and pitched and tossed as it came over the uneven ground. To sit in anything like a chair would have been foolish. A back rest would throw one forward in a frontward lurch, and give no support in case of a backward one. A sidewise tilt would tend to throw one out. Riding a ground car as if in a saddle was sense!

But Bordman was not so sure about the costume. The engineer opened the port and spoke hostilely out of it:

"D'you know there's a lady in this thing?"

The young Indian grinned. He waved his hand to Aletha, who pressed her nose against the viewport. And just then Bordman did understand the costume or lack of it. Air came in the open exit-port. It was hot and desiccated. It was furnace-like!

"How, 'Letha," called the ride on the caterwheel steed. "Either dress for the climate or put on a heat-suit before you come out of there!"

Aletha chuckled. Bordman heard a stirring behind him. Then Aletha climbed to the exit-port and swung out. Bordman heard a dour muttering from the engineer. Then he saw her greeting her cousin. She had slipped out of the conventionalized Amerind outfit to which Bordman was accustomed. Now she was clad as Anglo-Saxon girls dressed for beaches on the cool-temperature planets.

For a moment Bordman thought of sunstroke, with his own eyes dazzled by the still partly-filtered sunlight. But Aletha's Amerind coloring was perfectly suited to sunshine even of this intensity. Wind blowing upon her body would cool her skin. Her thick, straight black hair was at least as good protection against sunstroke as a heat-helmet. She might feel hot, but she would be perfectly safe. She wouldn't even sunburn. But he, Bordman. . . .

He grimly stripped to underwear and put on the heat-suit from his bag. He filled its canteens from the boat's water tank. He turned on the tiny, battery-powered motors. The suit ballooned out. It was intended for short periods of intolerable heat. The motors kept it inflated — away from the skin — and cooled its interior by evaporation of sweat plus water from its canteen tanks. It was a miniature air-conditioning system for one man, and it should enable him to endure temperatures otherwise lethal to someone with his skin and coloring. But it would use a lot of water.

He climbed to the exit port and went clumsily down the exterior ladder to the tail fin. He adjusted his goggles. He went over to the chattering young Indians, young man and girl, and held out his gloved hand.

"I'm Bordman," he said. "Here to make a degree-of-completion survey. What's wrong that we had to land by boat?"

Aletha's cousin shook hands cordially.

"I'm Ralph Redfeather," he said. "Project engineer. About everything's wrong. Our landing-grid's gone. We couldn't contact your ship in time to warn it off. It was in our gravity field before it answered, and its Lawlor drive couldn't take it away — not working because of the gravity stresses. Our power, of course, went with the landing-grid. The ship you came in can't get back, and we can't send a distress message anywhere, and our best estimation is that the colony will be wiped out — thirst and starvation — in six months. I'm sorry you and Aletha have to be included."

Then he turned to Aletha and said amiably:

"How's Mike Thundercloud and Sally Whitehorse and the

gang in general, 'Letha?"

The *Warlock* rolled on in her newly-established orbit about Xosa II. The landing boat was aground, having removed the two passengers. It would come back. Nobody on the ship wanted to stay around, because they knew the conditions and the situation below — unbearable heat and the complete absence of hope. But nobody had anything to do. The ship had been maintained in standard operating condition during its two months' voyage from Trent to here. No repairs or overhaulings were needed. There would be only standby watches until something happened, and nothing to do on those watches. There would be off-watch time for twenty-one out of every twenty-four hours, and no purposeful activity to fill even half an hour of it. In a matter of — probably — years, the *Warlock* should receive aid. She might be towed out of her orbit to space — five diameters out — in which the Lawlor drive could function, or the crew might simply be taken off. But meanwhile, those on board were as completely frustrated as the colony. They could not do anything at all to help themselves.

In one fashion the crewmen were worse off than the colonists. The colonists had at least the colorful prospect of death before them. They could prepare for it in their several ways. But the members of the *Warlock's* crew had nothing ahead but tedium. The skipper faced the future with extreme distaste.

The ride to the colony was torment. Aletha rode behind her cousin on the saddle blanket, and apparently suffered little if at all. But Bordman could only ride in the ground car's cargo space, along with the sack of mail from the ship. The ground was unbelievably rough and the jolting intolerable. The heat was literally murderous. In the metal cargo space, the temperature reached a hundred and sixty degrees in the sunshine — and given enough time, food would cook in no more heat than that. Of course a man had been known to enter an oven and stay there while a roast was cooked, and to come out alive. But the oven wasn't throwing him violently about or bringing sun heated — blue-white-sun heated — metal to press his heat-suit about him. The suit did make survival possible, but that was all. The contents of its canteens gave out just before arrival, and for a short time Bordman had only sweat for his suit to work with. It kept him alive by forced ventilation, but he arrived in a state of collapse. He drank the iced salt water they gave him and went to bed. He'd get back his strength with a proper sodium level in his blood. But he slept for twelve hours straight.

When he got up, he was physically normal again, but abysmally ashamed. It did no good to remind himself that Xosa II was rated minimum-comfort class D — a blue-white sun and a mean temperature of one hundred ten degrees. Africans could do steel construction work in the open, protected only by insulating shoes and gloves. But Bordman could not venture out-of-doors except in a heat-suit. He could not stay long then. It was not a weakness. It was a matter of genetics. But he was ashamed.

Aletha nodded to him when he found the Project Engineer's office. It occupied one of the hulls in which colony-establishment materials had been lowered by rocket power. There were forty of the hulls, and they had been emptied and arranged for inter-communication, so that an individual could change his quarters and ordinary associates from time to time and colony-fever — frantic irritation with one's companions — was minimized.

Aletha sat at a desk, busily making notes from a loose-leaf volume before her. The wall behind the desk was fairly lined with similar volumes.

"I made a spectacle of myself!" said Bordman.

"Not at all!" Aletha assured him. "It could happen to anybody. I wouldn't do too well on Timbuk."

There was no answer to that. Timbuk was essentially a jungle planet, barely emerging from the carboniferous stage. Its colonists thrived because their ancestors had lived on the shores of the Gulf of Guinea, on Earth. But Anglos did not find its climate healthful, nor would many other races. Amerinds died there quicker than most.

"Ralph's on the way here now," added Aletha. "He and Dr. Chuka were out picking a place to leave the records. The sanddunes here are terrible, you know. When an explorer ship does come to find out what's happened to us, these buildings could be covered up completely. Any place could be. It isn't easy to pick a record cache that's quite sure to be found."

"When," said Bordman, "there's nobody left alive to point it out. Is that it?"

"That's it," agreed Aletha. "It's pretty bad all around. I didn't plan to die just yet."

Her voice was perfectly normal. Bordman snorted. As a Senior Colonial Survey Officer, he'd been around. But he'd never yet known a human colony to be extinguished when it was properly equipped and after a proper pre-settlement survey. He'd seen panic, but never real cause for a matter-of-fact acceptance of doom.

There was a clanking noise outside the hulk which was the Project Engineer's headquarters. Bordman couldn't see clearly through the filtered port, so he reached over and opened the door. The brightness outside struck his eyes like a blow. He blinked them shut instantly and turned away. But he'd seen a glistening, caterwheel ground car stopping not far from the doorway.

He stood wiping tears from his light-dazzled eyes as footsteps sounded outside. Aletha's cousin came in, followed by a huge man with remarkably dark skin. The dark man wore eyeglasses with a curiously thick corklike nosepiece to insulate the necessary metal of the frame from his skin. It would blister if it touched bare flesh.

"This is Dr. Chuka," said Redfeather pleasantly. "Mr. Bordman. Dr. Chuka's the director of mining and mineralogy here."

Bordman shook hands with the ebony-skinned man. He grinned, showing startlingly white teeth. Then he began to shiver.

"It's like a freeze-box in here," he said in a deep voice. "I'll get a robe and be with you."

He vanished through a doorway, his teeth chattering audibly. Aletha's cousin took a half a dozen deliberate deep breaths and grimaced.

"I could shiver myself," he admitted, "but Chuka's really acclimated to Xosa. He was raised on Timbuk."

Bordman said curtly:

"I'm sorry I collapsed on landing. It won't happened again. I cane here to do a degree-of-completion survey that should open the colony to normal commerce, let the colonists' families move in, tourists, and so on. But I was landed by boat instead of normally, and I am told the colony is doomed. I would like an official statement to the degree of completion of the colony's facilities and an explanation of the unusual points I have just mentioned."

The Indian blinked at him. Then he smiled faintly. The dark man came back, zipping up an indoor warmth-garment. Redfeather dryly brought him up to date by repeating what Bordman had just said. Chuka grinned and sprawled comfortably in a chair.

"I'd say," he remarked, in that astonishing deep-toned voice of his, "I'd say sand got in your hair. And our colony. And the landing-grid. There's a lot of sand on Xosa. Wouldn't you say that was the trouble?"

The Indian said with deliberate gravity:

"Of course wind had something to do with it."

Bordman fumed.

"I think you know," he said, "that as a Senior Colonial Survey Officer, I have authority to give any orders needed for my work. I give one now. I want to see the landing-grid, if it is still standing. I take it that it didn't fall down?"

Redfeather flushed beneath the bronze pigment of his skin. It would be hard to offend a steelman more than to suggest that his work did not still stand up.

"I assure you," he said politely, "that it did not fall down."

"Your estimate of its degree of completion?"

"Eighty percent," said Redfeather.

"You've stopped work on it?"

"Work on it has been stopped," agreed the Indian.

"Even though the colony can receive no more supplies until it is completed?"

"Just so," said Redfeather without expression.

"Then I issue a formal order that I be taken to the landing-grid site immediately!" said Bordman angrily. "I want to see what sort of incompetence is responsible! Will you arrange it — at once?"

Redfeather said in a completely emotionless voice:

"You want to see the site of the landing-grid. Very good. Immediately."

He turned and walked out into the incredible, blinding sunshine. Bordman blinked at the momentary blast of light, and then began to pace up and down the office. He fumed. He was still ashamed of his collapse from the heat during the travel from the landed rocket-boat to the colony. Therefore he was touchy and irritable. But the order he had given was strictly justifiable.

He heard a small noise and whirled. Dr. Chuka, huge and black and spectacled, rocked back and forth in his seat, suppressing laughter.

"Now, what the devil does that mean?" demanded Bordman suspiciously. "It certainly isn't ridiculous to ask to see the structure on which the life of the colony fully depends!"

"Not ridiculous," said Dr. Chuka. "It's — hilarious!"

He boomed laughter in the office with the rounded ceiling of a remade robot hull. Aletha smiled with him, though her eyes were grave.

"You'd better put on a heat-suit," she said to Bordman.

He fumed again, tempted to defy all common sense because its dictates were not the same for everybody. But he marched away, back to the cubbyhole in which he had awakened. He donned the heat-suit that had not protected him adequately before, but had certainly saved his life, and filled the canteens topping full — he suspected he hadn't done so the last time. He went back to the

Project Engineer's office with a feeling of being burdened and absurd.

Out a filter-window, he saw that men with skins as dark as Dr. Chuka's were at work on a ground car. They were equipping it with a sunshade and curious shields like wings. Somebody pushed a sort of caterwheel handtruck toward it. They put big, heavy tanks into its cargo space. Dr. Chuka had disappeared, but Aletha was back at work making notes from the loose-leaf volume on the desk.

"May I ask," asked Bordman with some irony, "what your work happens to be just now?"

She looked up.

"I thought you knew!" she said in surprise. "I'm here for the Amerind Historical Society. I can certify coups. I'm taking coup-records for the Society. They'll go in the record cache Ralph and Dr. Chuka are arranging, so no matter what happens to the colony, the record of coups won't be lost."

"Coups?" demanded Bordman. He knew that Amerinds painted feathers on the key posts of steel structures they'd build, and he knew that the posting of such "coup-marks" was a cherished privilege and undoubtedly a survival or revival of some American Indian tradition back on Earth. But he did not know what they meant.

"Coups," repeated Aletha matter-of-factly. "Ralph wears three eagle-feathers. You saw them. He has three coups. Pinions, too! He built the landing-grids on Norlath and — Oh, you don't know!"

"I don't," admitted Bordman, his temper not of the best because of what seemed unnecessary condescension on Xosa II.

Aletha looked surprise.

"In the old days," she explained, "back on Earth, if a man scalped an enemy, he counted coup. The first to strike an enemy in battle counted coup, too — a lesser one. Nowadays a man counts coups for different things, but Ralph's three eagle-feathers mean he's entitled to as much respect as a warrior in the old days who, three separate times, had killed and scalped an enemy warrior in the middle of his own camp. And he is, too!"

Bordman grunted.

"Barbarous, I'd say!"

"If you like," said Aletha. "But it's something to be proud of — and one doesn't count coup for making a lot of money!" Then she paused and said curtly: "The word 'snobbish' fits it better than 'barbarous.' We are snobs! But when the head of a clan stands up in Council in the Big Teepee on Algonka, representing his clan, and men have to carry the ends of the feather headdress with all the coups the members of his clan have earned — why — one is proud to belong to that clan!" She added defiantly, "Even watching it on a vision-screen!"

Dr. Chuka opened the outer door. Blinding light poured in. He did not enter, and his body glistened with sweat.

"Ready for you, Mr. Bordman!"

Bordman adjusted his goggles and turned on the motors on his heat-suit. He went out the door.

The heat and light outside was like a blow. He darkened the goggles again and made his way heavily to the waiting, now-shaded ground car. He noted that there were other changes beside the sunshade. The cover deck of the cargo space was gone, and there were cylindrical riding seats like saddles in the back. The odd lower shields reached out sidewise from the body, barely above the caterwheels. He could not make out their purpose and irritably failed to ask.

"All ready," said Redfeather. "Dr. Chuka's coming with us. If you'll get in here, please . . ."

Bordman climbed awkwardly into the boxlike back of the car. He bestrode one of the cylindrical arrangements. With a saddle on it, it would undoubtedly have been a comfortable way to cover impossibly bad terrain in a mechanical carrier. He waited. About him there were the squatty hulls of the space barges which had been towed here by a colony ship, each one once equipped with rockets for landing. Emptied of their cargos, they had been huddled together into the three separate, adjoining communities. There were separate living-quarters and mess-halls and recreation-rooms for each, and any colonist lived in the community of his choice and shifted at pleasure, or visited, or remained solitary. For mental health a man has to be assured of his free will, and over-regimentation is deadly in any society. With men psychologically suited to colonize, it is fatal.

Above — but at a distance, now — was the monstrous strip of mountains, colored in glaring and unnatural tints. Immediately about there was raw rock. But it was peculiarly smooth, as if sand-grains had rubbed over it for uncountable aeons and carefully worn away every trace of unevenness. Half a mile to the left, dunes began and went away to the horizon. The nearer ones were small, but they gained in size with distance from the mountains — which evidently affected the surface-winds, hereabouts — and the edge of seeing was visibly not a straight line. The dunes yonder must be gigantic. But of course on a world the size of Earth, and which was waterless save for snow-patches at its poles, the size to which sand-dunes could grow had no limit. The surface of Xosa II was a sea of sand, on which islands and small continents of wind-swept rock were merely minor features.

Dr. Chuka adjusted a small metal object in his hand. It had a tube dangling from it. He climbed into the cargo space and fastened it to one of the two tanks previously loaded.

"For you," he told Bordman. "Those tanks are full of compressed air at rather high pressure — a couple of thousand pounds. Here's a reduction valve with an adiabatic expansion feature, to supply extra air to your heat-suit. It will be pretty cold, expanding from so high a pressure. Bring down the temperature a little more."

Bordman again felt humiliated. Chuka and Redfeather, because of their races, were able to move about nine-tenths naked in the open air on this planet, and they thrived. But he needed a special refrigerated costume to endure the heat. More, they provided him with sunshades and refrigerated air they did not need themselves. They were thoughtful of him. He was as much out of his element where they fitted perfectly, as he would have been making a degree-of-completion survey on an underwater project. He had to wear what was practically a diving suit and use a special air-supply to survive!

He choked down the irritation his own inadequacy produced.

"I suppose we can go now," he said as coldly as he could.

Aletha's cousin mounted the control saddle — though it was no more than a blanket — and Dr. Chuka mounted beside Bordman. The ground car got under way. It headed for the mountains.

The smoothness of the rock was deceptive. The caterwheel car lurched and bumped and swayed and rocked. It rolled and dipped and wallowed. Nobody could have remained in a normal seat on such terrain, but Bordman felt hopelessly undignified riding what amounted to a hobbyhorse. Under the sunshade it was infuriatingly like a horse on a carrousel. That there were three of them together made it look even more foolish. He stared about him, trying to take his mind from his own absurdity. His goggles made the light endurable, but he felt ashamed.

"Those side-fins," said Chuka's deep voice pleasantly, "the bottom ones, makes things better for you. The shade overhead cuts off direct sunlight, and they cut off the reflected glare. It would blister your skin even if the sun never touched you directly."

Bordman did not answer. The caterwheel car went on. It came to a patch of sand — tawny sand, heavily mineralized. There was a dune here. Not a big one for Xosa II, no more than a hundred feet high. But they went up its leeward, steeply slanting side. All the planet seemed to tilt insanely as the caterwheels spun. They reached the dune's crest, where it tended to curl over and break like a water-comber, and here the wheels struggled with sand precariously ready to fall, and Bordman had a sudden perception of the sands of Xosa II as the oceans that they really were. The dunes were waves which moved with infinite slowness, but the irresistible force of storm-seas. Nothing could resist them. Nothing!

They traveled over similar dunes for two miles. Then they began to climb the approaches to the mountains. And Bordman saw for the second time — the first had been through the ports of the landing boat — where there was a notch in the mountain wall and sand had flowed out of it like a waterfall, making a beautifully symmetrical cone-shaped heap against the lower cliffs. There were many such falls. In one place there was a sand-cascade. Sand had poured over a series of rocky steps, piling up on each in turn to its very edge, and then spilling again to the next.

They went up a crazily slanting spur of stone, whose sides were too steep for sand to lodge on, and whose narrow crest had a bare thin coating of powder.

The landscape looked like a nightmare. As the car went on, wobbling and lurching and dipping, the heights on either side made Bordman tend to dizziness. The coloring was impossible. The aridness, the desiccation, the lifelessness of everything about was somehow shocking. Bordman found himself straining his eyes for the merest, scrubbiest of bushes and for however stunted and isolated a wisp of grass.

The journey went on for an hour. Then there came a straining climb up a now-windswept ridge of eroded rock, and then the attainment of its highest point — and then the ground car went onward for a hundred yards and stopped.

They had reached the top of the mountain range, and there was doubtless another range beyond. But they could not see it. Here, at the place to which they had climbed so effortfully, there were no more rocks. There was no valley. There was no descending slope. There was sand. This was one of the sand-plateaus which were a unique feature of Xosa II. And Bordman knew, now, that the disputed explanation was the true one.

Winds, blowing over the mountains, carried sand as on other worlds they carried moisture and pollen and seeds and rain. Where two mountain ranges ran across the course of long-blowing winds, the winds eddied above the valley between. They dropped sand into it. The equivalent of trade winds, Bordman considered, in time would fill a valley to the mountain tops, just as trade winds provide moisture in equal quantity on other worlds, and civilizations have been built upon them. But —

"Well?" said Bordman challengingly.

"This is the site of the landing-grid," said Redfeather.

"Where?"

"Here," said the Indian. "A few months ago there was a valley here. The landing-grid had eighteen hundred feet of height built. There was to be four hundred feet more — the lighter top construction justifies my figure of eighty percent completion. Then there was a storm."

It was hot. Horribly, terribly hot, even here on a plateau at mountain top height. Dr. Chuka looked at Bordman's face and bent down in the vehicle. He turned a stopcock on one of the air tanks brought for Bordman's needs. Immediately Bordman felt cooler. His skin was dry, of course; the circulated air dried sweat as fast as it appeared. But he had the dazed, feverish feeling of a man in an artificial fever box. He'd been fighting it for some time. Now the coolness of the expanded air was almost deliriously refreshing.

Dr. Chuka produced a canteen. Bordman drank thirstily. The water was slightly salted to replace salt lost in sweat.

"A storm, eh?" asked Bordman, after a time of contemplation of his inner sensations as well as the scene of disaster before him. There'd be some hundreds of millions of tons of sand in even a section of this plateau. It was unthinkable that it could be removed except by a long-time sweep of changed trade winds along the length of the valley. "But what has a storm to do —?"

"It was a sandstorm," said Redfeather curtly. "Probably there was a sunspot flare-up. We don't know. But the pre-colonization survey spoke of sandstorms. The survey team even made estimates of sandfall in various places as so many inches per year. Here all storms drop sand instead of rain. But there must have been a sunspot flare because the storm blew for —" his voice went flat and deliberate because it was stating the unbelievable — "this storm blew for two months. We did not see the sun in all that time. And we couldn't work, naturally. So we waited it out. When it ended, there was a sand plateau where the survey had ordered the landing-grid to be built. The grid was under it. It is still under it. The top of eighteen hundred feet of steel is buried two hundred feet down in the sand you see. Our fabricated building-steel is piled ready for erection — under two thousand feet of sand. Without anything but stored power it is hardly practical" — Redfeather's tone was sardonic — "for us to try to dig it out. There are hundreds of millions of tons of stuff to be moved. If we could get the sand away, we could finish the grid. If we could finish the grid, we'd have power enough to get the sand away — in a few years, and if we could replace the machinery that wore out handling it. And if there wasn't another sandstorm."

He paused. Bordman took deep breaths of the cooler air. He could think more clearly.

"If you will accept photographs," said Redfeather, "you can check that we actually did the work."

Bordman saw the implications. The colony had been formed of Amerinds for the steel work and Africans for the labor. The Amerinds were congenitally averse to the handling of complex mining-machinery underground and the control of modern high speed smelting operations. Both races could endure this climate and work in it, provided that they had cooled sleeping-quarters. But they had to have power. Power not only to work with, but to live by. The air cooling machinery that made sleep possible also condensed from the cool air that minute trace of water-vapor it contained and that they needed for drink. But without power they would thirst. Without the landing-grid and the power it took from the ionosphere, they could not receive supplies from the rest of the universe. So they would starve.

Bordman said:

"I'll accept the photographs. I even accept the statement that the colony will die. I will prepare my report for the cache Aletha tells me you're preparing. And I apologize for any affront I may have offered you."

Dr. Chuka nodded. He regarded Bordman with benign warmth. Ralph Redfeather said cordially enough:

"That's perfectly all right. No harm done."

"And now," said Bordman, "since I have authority to give any orders needed for my work, I want to survey the steps you've taken to carry out those parts of your instructions dealing with emergencies. I want to see right away what you've done to beat this state of things. I know they can't be beaten, but I intend to leave a report on what you've tried!"

A fist-fight broke out in the crew's quarters within two hours after the *Warlock* had established its orbit — a first reaction to their catastrophe. The skipper went though the ship and painstakingly confiscated every weapon. He locked them up. He, himself, already felt the nagging effect of jangling nerves. There was nothing to do. He didn't know when there would ever be anything to do. It was a condition to produce hysteria.

It was night. Outside and above the colony there were uncountable myriads of stars. They were not the stars of Earth, of course, but Bordman had never been on Earth. He was used to unfamiliar constellations. He stared out a port at the sky, and noted that there were no moons. He remembered, when he thought, that Xosa II had no moons. There was a rustling of paper behind him. Aletha Redfeather turned a page in the loose-leaf volume and made a note. The wall behind her held many more such books. From them could be extracted the detailed history of every bit of work that had been done by the colony-preparation crews. Separate, tersely-phrased items could be assembled to make a record of individual men.

There had been incredible hardships, at first, and heroic feats. There had been an attempt to ferry water-supplies down from the pole by aircraft. It was not practical, even to build up a reserve of fluid. Winds carried sand particles here as on other worlds they carried moisture. Aircraft were abraded as they flew. The last working flier made a forced landing five hundred miles from the colony. A caterwheel expedition went out and brought the crew in. The caterwheel trucks were armored with silicone plastic, resistant to abrasion, but when they got back they had to be scrapped. Men had been lost in sudden sand squalls, and heroic searches made for them, and once or twice rescues. There had been cave-ins in the mines, and other accidents.

Bordman went to the door of the hull which was Ralph Redfeather's office. He opened it, and stepped outside.

It was like stepping into an oven. The sand was still hot from the sunshine just ended. The air was so utterly dry that Bordman instantly felt it sucking at the moisture of his nasal passages. In ten seconds his feet — clad in indoor footwear — were uncomfortably hot. In twenty the soles of his feet felt as if they were blistering. He would die of the heat even at night here! Perhaps he could endure the outside near dawn, but he raged a little. Here Amerinds and Africans lived and throve, but he could live unprotected for no more than an hour or two — and that at one special time of the planet's rotation!

He went back in, ashamed of the discomfort of his feet and angrily letting them scorch rather than admit to it.

Aletha turned another page.

"Look here!" said Bordman. "No matter what you say, you're going to go back on the *Warlock* before —"

She raised her eyes.

"We'll worry about that when the time comes. But I think not. I'd rather stay here."

"For the present, perhaps," snapped Bordman. "But before things get too bad you go back to the ship! They've rocket fuel enough for half a dozen landings of the landing boat. They can lift you out of here."

Aletha shrugged.

"Why leave here to board a derelict? The *Warlock's* practically that. What's your honest estimate of the time before a ship equipped to help us gets here?"

Bordman would not answer. He'd done some figuring. It had been a two-month journey from Trent, the nearest Survey base, to here. The *Warlock* had been expected to remain aground until the smelter it brought could load it with pig-metal. Which could be as little as two weeks, but would surprise nobody if it was two months instead. So the ship would be considered overdue for at least two months. It would be six months before anybody seriously wondered why it wasn't back with its cargo. There'd be a wait for lifeboats to come in, should there have been a mishap in space. Eventually a report of non-communication would be made to the Colonial Survey headquarters on Canna III. But it would take three months for that report to be received, and six more for a confirmation — even if ships made the voyages exactly at the most favorable intervals — and then there should at least be a complaint from the colony. There were lifeboats around on Xosa II, for emergency communication, and if a lifeboat didn't bring news of a planetary crisis, no crisis would be considered to exist. Nobody could imagine a landing-grid failing.

Maybe in a year somebody would think that maybe somebody ought to ask around about Xosa II. It would be much longer before somebody put a note on somebody else's desk that would suggest that when or if a suitable ship passed near Xosa II, or if one should be available for the inquiry, it might be worth while to have the non-communication from the planet looked into. Actually, to guess at three years before another ship arrived would be the most optimistic of estimates.

"You're a civilian," said Bordman. "When the food and water run low, you go back to the ship. You'll at least be alive when somebody does come to see what's the matter here!"

Aletha said mildly:

"Maybe I'd rather not be alive. Will you go back to the ship?"

Bordman flushed. He wouldn't. But he said:

"I can order you sent on board, and your cousin will carry out the order."

"I doubt it very much," said Aletha.

She returned to her task.

There were crunching footsteps outside the hulk. Bordman winced a little. With insulated sandals, it was normal for these colonists to move from one part of the colony to another in the open, even by daylight. He, Bordman, couldn't take out-of-doors at night!

Men came in. There were dark men with rippling muscles under glistening skin, and bronze Amerinds with coarse straight hair. Ralph Redfeather was with them. Dr. Chuka came in last of all.

"Here we are," said Redfeather. "These are our foremen. Among us, I think we can answer any questions you want to ask."

He made introductions. Bordman didn't try to remember the names. Abeokuta and Northwind and Sutata and Tallgrass and T'chka and Spottedhorse and Lewanika. . . . They were names which in combination would only be found in a very raw, new colony. But the men who crowded into the office were wholly at ease, in their own minds as well as in the presence of a Senior Colonial Survey Officer. They nodded as they were named, and the nearest shook hands. Bordman knew that he'd have liked their looks under other circumstances. But he was humiliated by the conditions on this planet. They were not. They were apparently only sentenced to death by them.

"I have to leave a report," said Bordman — and he was somehow astonished to know that he did expect to leave a report rather than make one: he accepted the hopelessness of the colony's future — "I have to leave a report on the degree-of-completion of the work here. But since there's an emergency, I have also to leave a report on the measures taken to meet it."

The report would be futile, of course. As futile as the coup-records Aletha was compiling, which would be read only after everybody on the planet was dead. But Bordman knew he'd write it. It was unthinkable that he shouldn't.

"Redfeather tells me," he added, "that the power in storage

can be used to cool the colony buildings — and therefore condense drinking water from the air — for just about six months. There is food for about six months also. If one lets the building warm up a little, to stretch the fuel, there won't be enough water to drink. Go on half rations to stretch the food, and there won't be enough water to last and the power will give out anyhow. No profit there!"

There were nods. The matter had been thrashed out long before.

"There's food in the *Warlock* overhead," Bordman went on, "but they can't use the landing boat more than a few times. It can't use ship fuel. No refrigeration to hold it stable. They couldn't land more than a ton of supplies all told. There are five hundred of us here. No help there!"

He looked from one to another.

"So we live comfortably," he told them with irony, "until our food and water and minimum night comfort run out together. Anything we do to try to stretch anything is useless because of what happens to something else. Redfeather tells me you accept the situation. What are you doing, since you accept it?"

Dr. Chuka said amiably.

"We've picked a storage place for our records, and our miners are blasting out space in which to put away the record of our actions to the last possible moment. It will be sand-proof. Our mechanics are building a broadcast unit we'll spare a tiny bit of fuel for. It will run twenty-odd years, broadcasting directions so it can be found regardless of how the terrain is changed by drifting sand."

"And," said Bordman, "the fact that nobody will be here to give directions."

Chuka added benignly.

"We're doing a great deal of singing, too. My people are — ah — religious. When we are no longer here — there have been boastings that there'll be a well-practiced choir ready to go to work in the next world."

White teeth showed in grins. Bordman was almost envious of men who could grin at such a thought. But he went on:

"And I understand that athletics have also been much practiced?"

Redfeather said:

"There's been time for it. Climbing teams have counted coup on all the worst mountains within three hundred miles. There's been a new record set for the javelin, adjusted for gravity constant, and Johnny Cornstalk did a hundred yards in eight point four seconds. Aletha has the records and has certified them."

"Very useful!" said Bordman sardonically. Then he disliked himself for saying it even before the bronze-skinned men's faces grew studiedly impassive.

Chuka waved his hand.

"Wait, Ralph! Lewanika's nephew will beat that within a week!"

Bordman was ashamed again because had spoken to cover up his own bad temper.

"I take it back," he said irritably. "What I said was uncalled for. I shouldn't have said it. But I came here to do a completion survey and what you've been giving me is material for an estimate of morale. It's not my line! I'm a technician, first and foremost. We're faced with a technical problem!"

Aletha spoke suddenly from behind him.

"But these are men, first and foremost, Mr. Bordman. And they're faced with a very human problem — how to die well. They seem to be rather good at it, so far."

Bordman ground his teeth. He was again humiliated. In his own fashion he was attempting the same thing. But just as he was genetically not qualified to endure the climate of this planet, he was not prepared for a fatalistic or pious acceptance of disaster. Amerind and African, alike, these men instinctively held to their own ideas of what the dignity of a man called upon him to do when he could not do anything but die. But Bordman's idea of his human dignity required him to be still fighting: still scratching at the eyes of fate or destiny when he was slain. It was in his blood or genes or the result of training. He simply could not, with self-respect, accept any physical situation as hopeless even when his mind assured him that it was.

"I agree," he said, "but I still have to think in technical terms. You might say that we are going to die because we cannot land the *Warlock* with food and equipment. We cannot land the *Warlock* because we have no landing-grid. We have no landing-grid because it and all the material to complete it is buried under millions of tons of sand. We cannot make a new, light-supply-ship type of landing-grid because we have no smelter to make beams, no power to run it if we had, yet if we had the beams we could get the power to run the smelter we haven't got to make the beams. And we have no smelter, hence no beams, no power, no prospect of food or help because we can't land the *Warlock*. It is strictly a circular problem. Break it at any point and all of it is solved."

One of the dark men muttered something under his breath to those near him. There were chuckles.

"Like Mr. Woodchuck," explained the man, when Bordman's eyes fell on him. "When I was a little boy there was a story like that."

Bordman said icily.

"The problem of coolness and water and food is the same sort of problem. In six months we could raise food — if we had power to condense moisture. We've chemicals for hydroponics — if we could keep the plants from roasting as they grew. Refrigeration and water and food are practically another circular problem."

Aletha said tentatively:

"Mr. Bordman —"

He turned, annoyed. Aletha said almost apologetically:

"On Chagan there was a — you might call it a woman's coup given to a woman I know. Her husband raises horses. He's mad about them. And they live in a sort of home on caterwheels out on the plains — the llanos. Sometimes they're months away from a settlement. And she loved ice cream and refrigeration isn't too simple. But she has a Doctorate in Human History. So she had her husband make an insulated tray on the roof of their prefabricated teepee, and she makes her ice cream there."

Men looked at her. Her cousin said amusedly:

"That should rate some sort of technical coup feather!"

"The Council gave her a brass pot — official," said Aletha. "Domestic science achievement." To Bordman she explained: "Her husband put a tray on the roof of their house, insulated from the heat of the house below. During the day there's an insulated cover on top of it, insulating it from the heat of the sun. At night she takes off the top cover, pours her custard, thin, in the tray. Then she goes to bed. She has to get up before daybreak to scrape it up, but by then the ice cream is frozen. Even on a warm night." She looked from one to another. "I don't know why. She said it was done in a place called Babylonia on Earth, many thousands of years ago."

Bordman blinked. Then he said:

"Damn! Who know how much the ground temperature drops here before dawn?"

"I do," said Aletha's cousin. "The top sand temperature falls forty-odd degrees. Warmer underneath, of course. But the air here is almost cool when the sun rises. Why?"

"Nights are cooler on all planets," said Bordman, "because every night the dark side radiates heat to empty space. There'd be frost everywhere every morning if the ground didn't store up heat during the day. If we prevent daytime heat storage — cover a patch of ground before dawn and leave it covered all day — and uncover it all night while shielding it from warm winds — we've got refrigeration! The night sky is empty space itself — two hundred eighty below zero!"

There was a murmur, then argument. The foremen of the Xosa II colony preparation crew were strictly practical men, but they had the habit of knowing why some things were practical. One does not do modern steel construction in contempt of theory, nor handle modern mining tools without knowing why as well as how they work. This proposal sounded like something that was based on reason — that should work to some degree. But how well? Anybody could guess that it should cool something at least twice as much as the normal night temperature drop. But somebody produced a slipstick and began to juggle it. Nobody paid much attention to Bordman. But there was a hum of discussion, in which Redfeather and Chuka were immediately included. By calculation, it appeared that if the air on Xosa II was really as clear as the bright stars and deep day sky color indicated, every second night a total drop of one hundred eighty degrees temperature could be secured by radiation to interstellar space — if there were no convection currents, and they could be prevented by —

It was the convection current problem which broke the assembly into groups with different solutions. But it was Dr. Chuka who boomed at all of them to try all three solutions and have them ready before daybreak, so the assembly left the hulk, still disputing enthusiastically. Somebody had recalled that there were dewponds in the one arid area on Timbuk, and somebody else remembered that irrigation on Delmos III was accomplished that same way. And they recalled how it was done. . . .

Voices went away in the oven-like night outside. Bordman grimaced, and again said:

"Darn! Why didn't I think of that myself?"

"Because," said Aletha, smiling, "you aren't a Doctor of Human History with a horse-raising husband and a fondness for ice cream. Even so, a technician was needed to break down the problems here into really simple terms." Then she said, "I think Bob Running Antelope might approve of you, Mr. Bordman."

Bordman fumed to himself.

"Who's he? — Just what does that whole comment mean?"

"I'll tell you," said Aletha, "when you've solved one or two more problems."

Her cousin came back into the room. He said with gratification:

"Chuka can turn out silicone-wool insulation, he says. Plenty of material, and he'll use a solar mirror to get the heat he needs. Plenty of temperature to make silicones! How much area will we need to pull in four thousand gallons of water a night?"

"How do I know?" demanded Bordman. "What's the moisture-content of the air here, anyhow?" Then he said, "Tell me! Are you using heat exchangers to help cool the air you pump into the buildings, before you use power to refrigerate it? It would save some power —"

The Indian project engineer said:

"Let's get to work on this! I'm a steel man myself, but —"

They settled down. Aletha turned a page.

The *Warlock* spun around the planet. The members of its crew withdrew into themselves. In even two months of routine tedious voyaging to this planet there had been the beginnings of irritation with the mannerisms of other men. Now there would be years of it. Within two days of its establishment in orbit, the *Warlock* was manned by men already morbidly resentful of fate, with the psychology of prisoners doomed to close confinement for an indeterminate but ghastly period. On the third day there was a second fist fight. A bitter one.

Fist flights are not healthy symptoms in a spaceship which cannot hope to make port for a matter of years.

Most human problems are circular and fall apart when a single trivial part of them is solved. There used to be enmity between races because they were different, and they tended to be different because they were enemies, so there was enmity. . . . The big problem of interstellar flight was that nothing could travel faster than light, and nothing could travel faster than light because mass increased with speed, and mass increased with speed — obviously! — because ships remained in the same time slot, and ships remained in the same time slot long after a one-second shift was possible because nobody realized that it meant traveling faster than light. And even before there was interstellar travel, there was practically no interplanetary commerce because it took so much fuel to take off and land. It took more fuel to carry the fuel to take off and land, and more still to carry the fuel for that, until somebody used power on the ground for heave-off instead of take-off, and again on the ground for landing. And then interplanetary ships carried cargos. On Xosa II there was an emergency because a sandstorm had buried the almost-completed landing-grid under some megatons of sand, and it couldn't be completed because there was only storage power because it wasn't completed, because there was only storage power because —

It took three weeks for the problem to be seen as the ultimate simple thing it really was. Bordman had called it a circular problem, but he hadn't seen its true circularity. It was actually — like all circular problems — inherently an unstable set of conditions. It began to fall apart simply because he saw that mere refrigeration would break its solidity.

In one week there were ten acres of desert covered with silicone-wool felt in great strips. By day a reflective surface was uppermost, and at sundown caterwheel trucks hooked on to towlines and neatly pulled it over on its back, to expose gridded black-body surfaces to the starlight. The gridding was precisely designed so that winds blowing across it did not make eddies in the grid squares. The chilled air in those pockets remained undisturbed, and there was no conduction of heat downward by eddy currents, while there was admirable radiation of heat out to space. This was in the manner of the night sides of all planets, only somewhat more efficient.

In two weeks there was a water yield of three thousand gallons per night, and in three weeks more there were similar grids over the colony houses and a vast roofed cooling shed for pre-chilling air to be used by the refrigeration systems themselves. The fuel store — stored power — was thereupon stretched to three times its former calculated usefulness. The situation was no longer a simple heat equation of despair.

Then something else happened. One of Dr. Chuka's assistants was curious about a certain mineral. He used the solar furnace that had made the silicone wool to smelt it. And Dr. Chuka saw him. After one blank moment he bellowed laughter and went to see Ralph Redfeather. Whereupon Amerind steel workers sawed apart a robot hull that was not longer a fuel tank because its fuel was gone, and they built a demountable solar mirror some sixty feet across — which African mechanics deftly powered — and suddenly there was a spot of incandescence even brighter than the sun of Xosa II, down on the planet's surface. It played upon a mineral cliff, and monstrous smells developed and even the African mining-technicians put on goggles because of the brightness. Presently there were little rolls of molten metal and slag trickling — and separating as they trickled — hesitantly down the cliffside. Dr. Chuka beamed and slapped his sweating thighs, and Bordman went out in a caterwheel truck, wearing a heat-suit, to watch it for all of twenty minutes. When he got back to the Project Engineer's office he gulped iced salt water and dug out the books he'd brought down from the ship. There was the spec-book for Xosa II, and the other volumes of definitions issued by the Colonial Survey. They were definitions of the exact meaning of terms used in briefer specifications, for items of equipment sometimes ordered by the Colony Office.

When Chuka came into the office presently, he carried the first crude pig of Xosa II iron in his gloved hand. He gloated. Bordman was then absent, and Ralph Redfeather worked feverishly at his desk.

"Where's Bordman?" demanded Chuka in that resonant bass voice of his. "I'm ready to report for degree-of-completion credit that the mining properties on Xosa II are prepared as of today to deliver pig iron, cobalt, zirconium and beryllium in commercial quantities. We require one day's notice to begin delivery of metal other than iron at the moment, because we're short of equipment, but we can furnish chromium and manganese on two days' notice — the deposits are farther away."

He dumped the pig of metal on the second desk, where Aletha sat with her perpetual loose-leaf volumes before her. The metal smoked and began to char the desktop. He picked it up again and tossed it from one gloved hand to the other.

"There y'are, Ralph!" he boasted. "You Indians go after your coups! Match this coup for me! Without fuel and minus all equipment except of our own making — I credit an assist on the mirror, but that's all — we're set to load the first ship that comes in for cargo! Now what are you going to do for the record? I think we've wiped your eye for you!"

Ralph hardly looked up. His eyes were very bright. Bordman had shown him and he was copying figures and formulae from a section of the definition book of the Colonial Survey. The book started with the specifications of antibiotic growth equipment for colonies with problems in local bacteria. It ended with definitions of the required strength of material and the designs stipulated for cages in zoos for motile fauna, sub-divided into carnivores, herbivores, and omnivores, with the special specifications for enclosures to contain abyssal creatures requiring extreme pressures, and the equipment for maintaining a healthfully re-poisoned atmosphere for creatures from methane planets.

Redfeather had the third volume open at, *"Landing Grids,*

*Lightest Emergency, Commerce Refuges, For Use Of."* There were some dozen of non-colonized planets along the most traveled space ways on which refuges for shipwrecked spacemen were maintained. Small forces of Patrol personnel manned them. Space lifeboats serviced them. They had the minimum installations which could draw on their planets' ionospheres for power, and they were not expected to handle anything bigger than a twenty ton lifeboat. But the specifications for the equipment of such refuges were included in the reference volumes for Bordman's use in making colonial surveys. They were compiled for the information of contractors who wanted to bid on Colonial Survey installations, and for the guidance of people like Bordman who checked up on the work. So they contained all the data for the building of a landing-grid, lightest, emergency, commerce-refuge type, for use of, in case of need. Redfeather copied feverishly.

Chuka ceased his boasting, but still he grinned.

"I know we're stuck, Ralph," he said, "but it's nice stuff to go in the records. Too bad we don't keep coup-records like you Indians."

Aletha's cousin — Project Engineer — said crisply:

"Go away! Who made your solar mirror? It was more than an assist! You get set to cast beams for us. Girders! I'm going to get a lifeboat aloft and away to Trent. Build a minimum size landing-grid! Build a fire under somebody so they'll send us a colony-ship with supplies. If there's not new sandstorm to bury the radiation refrigerators Bordman brought to mind, we can keep alive with hydroponics until the ship can arrive with something useful!"

Chuka stared.

"You don't mean we might actually live through this! Really?"

Aletha regarded the two of them with impartial irony.

"Dr. Chuka," she said, "you accomplished the impossible. Ralph, here, is planning to attempt the preposterous. Does it occur to you that Mr. Bordman is nagging himself to achieve the inconceivable? — It is inconceivable, even to him, but he's trying to do it."

"What's he trying to do?" demanded Chuka, wary but amused.

"He's trying," said Aletha, "to prove to himself that he's the best man on this planet. Because he's physically least capable of living here. His vanity's hurt. Don't underestimate him!"

"He's the best man here?" demanded Chuka blankly. "In his way he's all right. The refrigeration proves that. But he can't walk out-of-doors without a heat-suit!"

Ralph Redfeather, without ceasing his work, said:

"Nonsense, Aletha. He has courage. I give him that. But he couldn't walk a beam twelve hundred feet up. In his own way, yes. He's capable. But the best man —"

"I'm sure," agreed Aletha, "that he couldn't sing as well as the worst of your singing crew, Dr. Chuka, and any Amerind could outrun him. Even I could. But he's got something we haven't got, just as we have qualities he hasn't. We're secure in our competences. We knew what we can do, and that we can do it better than any —" her eyes twinkled — "than any paleface. But he doubts himself. All the time and in every way. And that's why he may be the best man on this planet. I'll bet he does prove it!"

Redfeather said scornfully:

"*You* suggested radiation refrigeration! What does it prove that he applied it?"

"That," said Aletha, "he couldn't face the disaster that was here without trying to do something about it — even when it was impossible. He couldn't face the deadly facts. He had to torment himself by seeing that they wouldn't be deadly if only this or that or the other were twisted a little. His vanity was hurt because nature had beaten men. His dignity was offended. And a man with easily-hurt dignity won't ever be happy, but he can be pretty good."

Chuka raised his ebony bulk from the chair in which he still shifted the iron pig from gloved hand to gloved hand.

"You're kind," he said, chuckling. "Too kind! I don't want to hurt his feelings. I wouldn't, for the world! But really — I've never heard a man praised for his vanity before, or admired for being touchy about his dignity! If you're right — why — it's been convenient. It might even mean hope. But — hm . . . would you want to marry a man like that?"

"Great Manitou forbid!" said Aletha firmly. She grimaced at the bare idea. "I'm an Amerind. I'll want my husband to be contented. I want to be contented along with him. Mr. Bordman will never be either happy or content. No paleface husband for me! But I don't think he's through here yet. Sending for help won't satisfy him. It's a further hurt to his vanity. He'll be miserable if he doesn't prove himself — to himself — a better man than that!"

Chuka shrugged his massive shoulders. Redfeather tracked down the last item he need and fairly bounced to his feet.

"What tonnage of iron can you get out, Chuka?" he demanded. "What can you do in the way of castings? What's the elastic modulus — how much carbon in this iron? And when can you start making castings? Big ones?"

"Let's go talk to my foreman," said Chuka. "We'll see how fast my — ah — mineral spring is trickling metal down the cliff face. If you can really launch a lifeboat, we might get some help here in a year and a half instead of five. . . ."

They went out-of-doors together. There was a small sound in the next office. Aletha was suddenly very still. She sat motionless for a long half minute. Then she turned her head.

"I owe you an apology, Mr. Bordman," she said ruefully. "It won't take back the discourtesy, but — I'm very sorry."

Bordman came into the office from the next room. He was rather pale. He said wryly:

"Eavesdroppers never hear good of themselves, eh? — Actually I was on the way in here when I heard — references to myself. It would embarrass Chuka and your cousin to know I heard. So, I stopped. Not to listen, but to keep them from knowing I'd heard their private opinions of me. I'll be obliged if you don't tell them. They're entitled to their opinions of me. I've mine of them." He added. "Apparently I think more highly of them than they do of me!"

"It must have sounded horrible!" Aletha said. "But they — we — all of us think better of you than you do of yourself!"

Bordman shrugged.

"You in particular. Would you marry someone like me? Great Manitou, no!"

"For an excellent reason," said Aletha. "When I get back from here — *if* I get back from here — I'm going to marry Bob Running Antelope. He's nice. I like the idea of marrying him. But I look forward not only to happiness but to contentment. To me that's important. It isn't to you, or to the woman you ought to marry. And I — well — I simply don't envy either of you a bit."

"I see!" said Bordman with irony. He didn't. "I wish you all the contentment you look for." Then he snapped: "But what's this business about expecting more from me? What spectacular idea do you expect me to pull out of somebody's hat now? — Because I'm frantically vain?"

"I haven't the least idea," said Aletha. "But I think you'll come up with something we couldn't possibly imagine. And I didn't say it was because you were vain, but because you are discontented with yourself. It's born in you. And there you are!"

"If you mean neurotic," snapped Bordman, "you're all wrong. I'm not neurotic. I'm hot, and I'm annoyed. I'll get hopelessly behind schedule because of this mess. But that's all!"

Aletha stood up and shrugged her shoulders ruefully.

"I repeat my apology," she told him, "and leave you the office. But I also repeat that I think you'll turn up something nobody else expects — and I've no idea what it will be. But you'll do it now to prove that I'm wrong about how your mind works."

She went out. Bordman clamped his jaws tightly. He felt that especially haunting discomfort which comes from suspecting that one has been told something about oneself which may be true.

"Idiotic!" he fumed, all alone. "Me neurotic? Me wanting to prove I'm the best man here out of vanity?" He made a scornful noise. He sat impatiently at the desk. "Absurd!" he muttered. "Why should I need to prove to myself I'm capable? What would I do if I felt such a need, anyhow?"

Scowling, he stared at the wall. It was a nagging sort of question. What would he do if she were right? If he did need constantly to prove to himself —

He stiffened, suddenly. A look of intense surprise came upon his face. He'd thought of what a self-doubtful, discontented man would try to do, here on Xosa II at this juncture.

The surprise was because he also thought of how it could be done.


The *Warlock* came to life. Her skipper gloomily answered the emergency call from Xosa II. In a minute he clicked off the communicator and hastened to an exterior port, deeply darkened against those times when the blue-white sun Xosa shone upon this side of the hull. He moved the manual control to make it more transparent, and stared down at the monstrous, tawny, mottled surface of the planet five thousand miles away. He searched for the spot he knew was the colony's site.

He saw what he'd been told he'd see. It was an infinitely fine, threadlike projection from the surface of the planet. It rose at a slight angle — it leaned toward the planet's west — and it expanded and widened and formed an extraordinary sort of mushroom-shaped object that was completely impossible. It could not be. Humans do not create visible objects twenty miles high, which at their tops expand like toadstools on excessively slender stalks, and which drift westward, fray, and grow thin, and are constantly renewed.

But it was true. The skipper of the *Warlock* gazed until he was completely sure. It was no atomic bomb, because it continued to exist. It faded, but was constantly replenished. There was no such thing!

He went through the ship, bellowing, and faced mutinous snarlings. But when the *Warlock* was around on that side of the planet again, the members of the crew saw the strange appearance, too. They examined it with telescopes. They grew hysterical. They went frantically to work to clear away the signs of a month and a half of mutiny and despair.

It took them three days to get the ship to tidiness again, and during all that time the peculiar tawny jet remained. On the sixth day the jet was fainter. On the seventh it was larger than before. It continued larger. And telescopes at highest magnification verified what the emergency communication had said.

Then the crew began to experience frantic impatience. It was worse, waiting those last three or four days, than even all the hopeless time before. But there was no reason to hate anybody now. The skipper was very much relieved.

Eighteen hundred feet of steel grid soared overhead. It made a crisscross, ring-shaped wall more that a quarter mile high and almost to the top of the surrounding mountains. But the valley was not exactly a normal one. It was a crater, now: a steeply sloping, conical pit whose walls descended smoothly to the red painted, glistening steel structure. More girders for the completion of the grid projected from the sand just outside its circle. And in the landing-grid there was now a smaller, elaborate, truss-braced object. It rested on the rocky ground, unpainted and quite small. A hundred feet high, perhaps, and no more than three hundred across. But it was visibly a miniature of the great, newly-uncovered, repainted landing-grid which was qualified to handle interstellar cargo ships and all the proper space-traffic of a minerals colony planet.

A caterwheel truck came lurching and rolling and rumbling down the side of the pit. It had a sunshade and ground reflector wings, and Bordman slouched on a hobby-horse saddle in its back cargo section. He wore a heat-suit.

The truck reached the pit's bottom and bumped up to a tool-shed and stopped. Bordman got out, visibly cramped by the jolting, rocking, exhausting ride.

"Do you want to go in the shed and cool off?" asked Chuka.

"I'm all right," said Bordman. "I'm quite comfortable, so long as you feed me that expanded air." It was plain that he resented needing even a special air-supply. "What's all this about? Bringing the *Warlock* in? Why the insistence of my being here?"

"Ralph has a problem," said Chuka blandly. "He's up there —

See? He needs you. There's a hoist. You've got to check degree-of-completion anyhow. You might take a look around while you're up there. But he's anxious for you to see something. There where you see the little knot of people. The platform."

Bordman grimaced. When one was well started on a survey, one got used to heights and depths and all sorts of environments. But he hadn't been up on steel work in a good many months. Not since the survey on Kalka IV nearly a year ago. He would be dizzy at first.

He accompanied Chuka to the spot where a steel cable dangled from an almost invisibly thin beam high above. There was a strictly improvised cage to ascend in — planks and a hand rail forming an insecure platform that might hold four people. He got into it, and Dr. Chuka got in beside him. Chuka waved his hand. The cage started up.

Bordman winced as the ground dropped away below. It was ghastly to be dangling in emptiness like this. He wanted to close his eyes. The cage went up and up. It took many long minutes to reach the top.

There was a newly-made platform there. The sunlight was blindingly bright, the landscape an intolerable glare. Bordman adjusted his goggles to maximum darkness and stepped gingerly from the swaying cage to the hardly more solid-seeming area. Here he was in midair on a platform barely ten feet square. It was rather more than twice the height of a metropolitan skyscraper from the ground. The mountain-crests were only half a mile away and not much higher. Bordman was acutely uncomfortable. He would get used to it, but —

"Well?" he asked. "Chuka said you needed me here. What's the matter?"

Ralph Redfeather nodded formally. Aletha was here, too, and two of Chuka's foremen — one did not look happy — and four of the Amerind steel-workers. They grinned at Bordman.

"I wanted you to see," said Aletha's cousin, "before we threw on the current. It doesn't look like that little grid could handle the sand it took care of. But Lewanika wants to report."

A dark man who worked under Chuka — and looked as if he belonged on solid ground — said:

"We cast the beams for the small landing-grid, Mr. Bordman. We melted the metal out of the cliffs and ran it into moulds as it flowed down."

He stopped. One of the Indians said:

"We made the girders into the smaller landing-grid. It bothered us because we built it on the sand that had buried the big grid. We didn't understand why you ordered it there. But we built it."

The second dark man said with a trace of swagger:

"We made the coils, Mr. Bordman. We made the small grid so it would work the same as the big one when it was finished. And then we made the big grid work, finished or not!"

Bordman said impatiently:

"All right. Very good. But what is this? A ceremony?"

"Just so," said Aletha, smiling. "Be patient, Mr. Bordman!"

Her cousin said:

"We built the small grid on the top of the sand. And it tapped the ionosphere for power. No lack of power then! And we'd set it to heave up sand instead of ships. Not to heave it out into space, but to give it up to a mile a second vertical velocity. Then we turned it on."

"And we rode it down, that little grid," said one of the remaining Indians, grinning. "What a party! Manitou!"

Redfeather frowned at him and took up the narrative.

"It hurled the sand up from its center, as you said it would. The sand swept air with it. It made a whirlwind, bringing more sand from outside the grid into its field. It was a whirlwind with fifteen megakilowatts of power to drive it. Some of the sand went twenty miles high. Then it made a mushroom head and the winds up yonder blew it to the west. It came down a long way off, Mr. Bordman. We've made a new dune area ten miles downwind. And the little grid sank as the sand went away from around it. We had to stop it three times, because it leaned. We had to dig under parts of it to get it straight up again. But it went down into the valley."

Bordman turned up the power to his heat-suit motors. He felt uncomfortably warm.

"In six days," said Ralph, almost ceremonially, "it had uncovered half the original grid we'd built. Then we were able to modify that to heave sand and to let it tap the ionosphere. We were able to use a good many times the power the little grid could apply to sand lifting. In two days more the landing-grid was clear. The valley bottom was clean. We shifted some hundreds of millions of tons of sand by landing-grid, and now it is possible to land the *Warlock*, and receive her supplies. The solar-power furnace is already turning out pigs for her loading. We wanted you to see what we have done. The colony is no longer in danger, and we shall have the grid completely finished for your inspection before the ship is ready to return."

Bordman said uncomfortably:

"That's very good. It's excellent. I'll put it in my survey report."

"But," said Ralph, more ceremonially still, "we have the right to count coup for the members of our tribe and clan. Now —"

Then there was confusion. Aletha's cousin was saying syllables that did not mean anything at all. The other Indians joined in at intervals, speaking gibberish. Aletha's eyes were shining and she looked pleased and satisfied.

"What — what's this?" demanded Bordman when they stopped.

Aletha spoke proudly.

"Ralph just formally adopted you into the tribe, Mr. Bordman — and into his clan and mine! He gave you a name I'll have to write down for you, but it means, 'Man-who-believes-not-his-own-wisdom.' And now —"

Ralph Redfeather, licensed interstellar engineer, graduate of the stiffest technical university in this quarter of the galaxy, wearer of three eagle-pinion feathers and clad in a pair of insulated sandals and a breechcloth — Ralph Redfeather whipped out a small paint-pot and a brush from somewhere and began carefully to paint on a section of girder ready for the next tier of steel. He painted a feather on the metal.

"It's a coup," he told Bordman over his shoulder. "Your coup. Placed where it was earned — up here. Aletha is authorized to certify it. And the head of the clan will add an eagle feather to the headdress he wears in Council in the Big Tepee on Algonka, and — your clan-brothers will be proud."

Then he straightened up and held out his hand.

Chuka said benignly:

"Being civilized men, Mr. Bordman, we Africans do not go in for uncivilized feathers. But we — ah — rather approve of you too. And we plan a corroboree at the colony after the *Warlock* is down, when there will be some excellently practiced singing. There is — ah — a song, a sort of choral calypso, about this adventure you have brought to so satisfying a conclusion. It is quite a good calypso. It's likely to be popular on a good many planets."

Bordman swallowed. He felt that he ought to say something, and he did not know what.

But just then there was a deep-toned humming in the air. It was a vibrant tone, instinct with limitless power. It was the eighteen-hundred-foot landing-grid, giving off that profoundly bass and vibrant note it uttered while operating. Bordman looked up.

The *Warlock* was coming down.

After Bordman made his report he found that the newest graduates of Space Survey training had been swallowed up by the needs of the service, and he was apparently needed as badly as before. But he protested vigorously, and went back to Lani III and enjoyed the society of Riki and his children for a full year and a half.

Then three Senior Officers died within one year, and the Survey's facilities were stretched to the breaking-point. Population-pressure required the opening of colonies. The safety of thousands and millions of human lives depended on the Survey's work. Worlds which had been biologically surveyed had also to be checked to make sure they were equipped to sustain the populations waiting impatiently to swarm upon them.

Reluctantly, to meet the emergency, Bordman agreed to return to the Service for one year only.

But he'd served seven, with only two brief visits to his children and his wife, when he was promised that after the checking of a single robot colony on Loren Two, his resignation would be accepted.

So he boarded a Crete Line Ship for his last active assignment in the Colonial Survey. . . .

# III

## COMBAT TEAM

The nearer moon went by overhead. It was jagged and irregular in shape, probably a captured asteroid. Huyghens had seen it often enough, so he did not go out of his quarters to watch it hurtle across the sky with seemingly the speed of an atmosphere-flier, occulting the stars as it went. Instead, he sweated over paperwork, which should have been odd because he was technically a felon and all his labors on Loren Two felonious. It was odd, too, for a man to do paperwork in a room with steel shutters and a huge bald eagle — untethered — dozing on a three-inch perch set in the wall. But paperwork was not Huyghens' real task. His only assistant had tangled with a night-walker, and the furtive Kodius Company ships had taken him away to where Kodius Company ships came from. Huyghens had to do two men's work in loneliness. To his knowledge, he was the only man in the solar system.

Below him, there was snuffling. Sitka Pete got up heavily and padded to his water-pan. He lapped the refrigerated water and sneezed. Sourdough Charley waked and complained in a rumbling growl. There were divers other rumblings and mutterings below. Huyghens called reassuringly, "Easy there!" and went on with his work. He finished a climate report, and fed figures to a computer. While it hummed over them he'd entered the inventory totals in the station log, showing what supplies remained. Then he began to write up the log proper.

*"Sitka Pete,"* he wrote, *"has apparently solved the problem of killing individual sphexes. He has learned that it doesn't do to hug them and that his claws can't penetrate their hide, not the top-hide, anyhow. Today Semper notified us that a pack of sphexes had found the scent-trail to the station. Sitka hid downwind until they arrived. Then he charged the rear and brought his paws together on both sides of the sphex's head in terrific pair of slaps. It must have been like two twelve-inch shells arriving from opposite directions at the same time. It must have scrambled the sphex's brains as if they were eggs. It dropped dead. He killed two more with such mighty pairs of wallops. Sourdough Charley watched, grunting, and when the sphexes turned on Sitka, he charged in his turn. I, of course, couldn't shoot too close to him, so he might have fared badly except that Faro Nell came pouring out of the bear-quarters to help. The diversion enabled Sitka Pete to resume the use of his new technique, towering on his hind legs*

*and swinging his paws in the new and grisly fashion. The fight ended promptly. Semper flew and screamed above the scrap, but as usual did not join in. Note: Nugget, the cub, tried to mix in but his mother cuffed him out of the way. Sourdough and Sitka ignored him as usual. Kodius Champion's genes are sound!"*

The noises of the night went on outside. There were notes like organ-tones — song lizards. There were tittering, giggling cries of the night-walkers. There were sounds like tack-hammers, and doors closing, and from every direction came noises like hic-coughs in various keys. These were made by the improbable small creatures which on Loren Two took the place of insects.

Huyghens wrote out:

*"Sitka seemed ruffled when the fight was over. He used his trick on the head of every dead or wounded sphex, except those he'd killed with it, lifting up their heads for his pile-driver-like blows from two directions at once, as if to show Sourdough how it was done. There was much grunting as they hauled the carcasses to the incinerator. It almost seemed —"*

The arrival-bell clanged, and Huyghens jerked up his head to stare at it. Semper, the eagle, opened icy eyes. He blinked.

Noises. There was a long, deep, contented snore from below. Something shrieked, out in the jungle. Hiccoughs, clatterings, and organ-notes. . . .

The bell clanged again. It was a notice that an unscheduled ship aloft somewhere had picked up the beacon-beam — which only Kodius Company ships should know about — and was com-municating for a landing. But there shouldn't be any ships in this solar system just now! The Kodius Company's colony was com-pletely illegal, and there were few graver crimes than unautho-rized occupation of a new planet.

The bell clanged a third time. Huyghens swore. His hand went out to cut off the beacon, and then stopped. That would be useless. Radar would have fixed it and tied it in with physical fea-tures like the nearby sea and the Sere Plateau. The ship could find the place, anyhow, and descend by daylight.

"The devil!" said Huyghens. But he waited yet again for the bell to ring. A Kodius Company ship would double-ring to reas-sure him. But there shouldn't be a Kodius Company ship for months.

The bell clanged singly. The space-phone dial flickered and a voice came out of it, tinny from stratospheric distortion:

*"Calling ground. Calling ground. Crete Line ship Odysseus calling ground on Loren Two. Landing one passenger by boat. Put on*

*your field lights."*

Huyghens' mouth dropped open. A Kodius Company ship would be welcome. A Colonial Survey ship would be extremely unwelcome, because it would destroy the colony and Sitka and Sourdough and Faro Nell and Nugget — and Semper — and carry Huyghens off to be tried for unauthorized colonization and all that it implied.

But a commercial ship, landing one passenger by boat. . . . There were simply no circumstances under which that could happen. Not to an unknown, illegal colony. Not to a furtive station!

Huyghens flicked on the landing-field lights. He saw the glare over the field half a mile away. Then he stood up and prepared to take the measures required by discovery. He packed the paper-work he'd been doing into the disposal-safe. He gathered up all personal documents and tossed them in. Every record, every bit of evidence that the Kodius Company maintained this station went into the safe. He slammed the door. He moved his finger toward the disposal-button, which would destroy the contents and melt down even the ashes past their possible use for evidence in court.

Then he hesitated. If it were a Survey ship, the button had to be pressed and he himself must resign himself to a long term in prison. But a Crete Line ship — if the space-phone told the truth — was not threatening. It was simply unbelievable.

He shook his head. He got into travel garb, armed himself, and went down into the bear-quarters, turning on lights as he went. There were startled snufflings, and Sitka Pete reared himself to a sitting position to blink at him. Sourdough Charley lay on his back with his legs in the air. He'd found it cooler, sleeping that way. He rolled over with a thump, and made snorting sounds which somehow sounded cordial. Faro Nell padded to the door of her separate apartment, assigned to her so that Nugget would not be underfoot to irritate the big males.

Huyghens, as the human population of Loren Two, faced the work-force, fighting-force, and — with Nugget — four-fifths of the terrestrial non-human population of the planet. They were mutated Kodiak bears, descendants of that Kodius Champion for whom the Kodius Company was named. Sitka Pete was a good twenty-two hundred pounds of lumbering, intelligent carnivore, Sourdough Charley would weigh within a hundred pounds of that figure. Faro Nell was eighteen hundred pounds of female charm and ferocity. Then Nugget poked his muzzle around his mother's furry rump to see what was toward, and he was six hundred pounds of ursine infancy. The animals looked at Huyghens expectantly. If he'd had Semper riding on his shoulder they'd have known what was expected of them.

"Let's go," said Huyghens. "It's dark outside, but somebody's coming. And it may be bad!"

He unfastened the outer door of the bear-quarters. Sitka Pete went charging clumsily through it. A forthright charge was the best way to develop any situation — if one was an oversized male Kodiak bear. Sourdough went lumbering after him. There was nothing hostile immediately outside. Sitka stood up on his hind legs — he reared up a solid twelve feet — and sniffed the air. Sourdough methodically lumbered to one side and then the other, sniffing in his turn. Nell came out, nine-tenths of a ton of daintiness, and rumbled admonitorily at Nugget, who trailed her closely. Huyghens stood in the doorway, his night-sighted gun ready. He felt uncomfortable at sending the bears ahead into a Loren Two jungle at night, but they were qualified to scent danger, and he was not.

The illumination of the jungle was a wide path toward the landing-field, made for weirdness of the look of things. There were arching giant ferns and columnar trees which grew above them, and the extraordinary lanceolate underbrush of the jungle. The flood-lamps, set level with the ground, lighted everything from below. The foliage, then, was brightly lit against the black night-sky, brightly enough lit to dim the stars.

"On ahead!" commanded Huyghens, waving. "Hup!"

He swung the bear-quarters door shut, and moved toward the landing-field through the lane of lighted forest. The two giant male Kodiaks lumbered ahead. Sitka Pete dropped to all fours and prowled. Sourdough Charley followed closely, swinging from side to side. Huyghens came behind the two of them, and Faro Nell brought up the rear with Nugget nudging her.

It was an excellent military formation for progress through dangerous jungle. Sourdough and Sitka were advance guard and point, respectively, while Faro Nell guarded the rear. With Nugget to look after, she was especially alert against attack from behind. Huyghens was, of course, the striking force. His gun fired explosive bullets which would discourage even sphexes, and his night-sight — a cone of light which went on when he took up the trigger-slack — told exactly where they would strike. It was not a sportsmanlike weapon, but the creatures of Loren Two were not sportsmanlike antagonists. The night-walkers, for example. But night-walkers feared light. They attacked only in a species of hysteria if it were too bright.

Huyghens moved toward the glare of the landing field. His mental state was savage. The Kodius Company on Loren Two was completely illegal. It happened to be necessary, from one point of view, but it was still illegal. The tinny voice on the space-phone was not convincing, in ignoring that illegality. But if a ship landed, Huyghens could get back to the station before men could follow, and he'd have the disposal-safe turned on in time to protect those who'd sent him here.

Then he heard the faraway and high harsh roar of a landing boat rocket — not a ship's bellowing tubes — as he made his way through the unreal-seeming brush. The roar grew louder as he pushed on, the three Kodiaks padding here and there, sniffing for danger.

He reached the edge of the landing field, and it was blindingly bright, with the customary divergent beams slanting skyward so a ship could check its instrument-landing by sight. Landing fields like this had been standard, once upon a time. Nowadays all developed planets had landing-grids — monstrous structures which drew upon ionospheres for power and lifted and drew down starships with remarkable gentleness and unlimited force. This sort of landing field would now be found only where a survey-team of ecology or bacteriology was under way, or where a newly authorized colony had not yet been able to build its landing-grid. Of course, it was unthinkable that anybody would attempt a settlement in defiance of the law!

Already, as Huyghens reached the edge of the scorched open space, the night-creatures had rushed to the light, like moths on Earth. The air was misty with crazily gyrating, tiny flying things. They were innumerable and of every possible form and size, from the white midges of the night and multi-winged flying worms to those revoltingly naked-looking larger creatures which might have passed for plucked flying monkeys if they had not been carnivorous and worse. They flying things soared and whirred and danced and spun insanely in the glare, making peculiarly plaintive humming noises. They almost formed a lamp-lit ceiling over the cleared space, and actually did hide the stars. Staring upward, Huyghens could just barely make out the blue-white flame of the space-boat's rocket through the fog of wings and bodies.

The rocket-flame grew steadily in size. Once it tilted to adjust the boat's descending course. It went back to normal. A speck of incandescence at first, it grew until it was like a great star, then a more-than-brilliant moon, and then it was a pitiless glaring eye.

Huyghens averted his gaze from it. Sitka Pete sat lumpily and blinked at the dark jungle away from the light. Sourdough ignored the deepening, increasing rocket-roar. He sniffed the air. Faro Nell held Nugget firmly under one huge paw and licked his head as if tidying him up to be seen by company. Nugget wriggled.

The roar became that of ten thousand thunders. A warm breeze blew outward from the landing field. The rocket-boat hurtled downward, and as its flame touched the mist of flying things, they shriveled and burned. Then there were churning clouds of dust everywhere, and the center of the field blazed terribly — and something slid down a shaft of fire, squeezed it flat, and sat on it — and the flame went out. The rocket-boat sat there, resting on its tail-fins, pointing toward the stars from which it came.

There was a terrible silence after the tumult. Then, very faintly, the noises of the night came again. There were sounds like those of organ-pipes, and very faint and apologetic noises like hiccoughs. All these sounds increased, and suddenly Huyghens could hear quite normally. As he watched, a side-port opened with a clattering, something unfolded from where it had been inset into the hull of the space-boat, and there was a metal passageway across the flame-heated space on which the boat stood.

A man came out of the port. He reached back in and shook hands. Then he climbed down the ladder-rungs to the walkway, and marched above the steaming baked area, carrying a traveling bag. At the end of the walk he stepped to the ground, and moved hastily to the edge of the clearing. He waved to the space-boat. The walkway folded briskly back up to the hull and vanished into it, and almost at once a flame exploded into being under the tail-fins. There were fresh clouds of monstrous, choking dust, a brightness like that of a sun, and noise past the possibility of endurance. Then the light rose swiftly through the dust-cloud, sprang higher, and climbed more swiftly still. When Huyghens' ears again permitted him to hear anything, there was only a diminished mutter in the heavens and a faint bright speck of light ascending to the sky, swinging eastward as it rose to intercept the ship from which it had descended.

The night-noises of the jungle went on, even though there was a spot of incandescence in the day-bright clearing, and steam rolled up in clouds at the edge of the hottest area. Beyond that edge, a man with a traveling bag in his hand looked about him.

Huyghens advanced toward him as the incandescence dimmed. Sourdough and Sitka preceded him. Faro Nell trailed faithfully, keeping a maternal eye on her offspring. The man in the clearing stared at the parade they made. It would be upsetting, even after preparation, to land at night on a strange planet, to have the ship's boat and all links to the rest of the cosmos depart, and then to find oneself approached — it might seemed stalked — by two colossal male Kodiak bears, with a third bear and a cub behind them. A single human figure in such company might seem irrelevant.

The new arrival gazed blankly. He moved back a few steps. Then Huyghens called:

"Hello, there! Don't worry about the bears! They're friends!"

Sitka reached the newcomer. He went warily downwind from him and sniffed. The smell was satisfactory. Man-smell. Sitka sat down with the solid impact of more than a ton of bear-meat landing on packed dirt, and regarded the man. Sourdough said *"Whoosh!"* and went on to sample the air beyond the clearing. Huyghens approached. The newcomer wore the uniform of the Colonial Survey. That was bad. It bore the insignia of a senior officer. Worse.

"Hah!" said the just-landed man. "Where are the robots? What in all the nineteen hells are these creatures? Why did you shift your station? I'm Bordman, here to make a progress-report on your colony."

Huyghens said:

"What colony?"

"Loren Two Robot Installation —" Then Bordman said indignantly, "Don't tell me that that idiot skipper can have dropped me at the wrong place! This is Loren Two, isn't it? And this is the landing field. But where are your robots? You should have the beginning of a grid up! What the devil's happened here and what are these beasts?"

Huyghens grimaced.

"This," he said, "is an illegal, unlicensed settlement. I'm a criminal. These beasts are my confederates. If you don't want to associate with criminals you needn't, of course, but I doubt if you'll live till morning unless you accept my hospitality while I think over what to do about your landing. In reason, I ought to shoot you."

Faro Nell came to a halt behind Huyghens, which was her proper post in all outdoor movement. Nugget, however, saw a new human. Nugget was a cub, and therefore friendly. He ambled forward. He wriggled bashfully as he approached Bordman. He sneezed, because he was embarrassed.

His mother overtook him and cuffed him to one side. He wailed. The wail of a six-hundred-pound Kodiak bear-cub is a remarkable sound. Bordman gave ground a pace.

"I think," he said carefully, "that we'd better talk things over. But if this is an illegal colony, of course, you're under arrest and anything you say will be used against you."

Huyghens grimaced again.

"Right," he said. "But now if you'll walk close to me, we'll head back to the station. I'd have Sourdough carry your bag — he likes to carry things — but he may need his teeth. We've half a mile to travel." He turned to the animals. "Let's go!" he said commandingly. "Back to the station! Hup!"

Grunting, Sitka Pete arose and took up his duties as advance point of a combat-team. Sourdough trailed, swinging widely to one side and another. Huyghens and Bordman moved together. Faro Nell and Nugget brought up the rear.

There was only one incident on the way back. It was a night-walker, made hysterical by the lane of light. It poured through the underbrush, uttering cries like maniacal laughter.

Sourdough brought it down, a good ten yards from Huyghens.

When it was over, Nugget bristled up to the dead creature, uttering cub-growls. He feigned to attack it.

His mother whacked him soundly.

There were comfortable, settling-down noises below, as the bears grunted and rumbled, and ultimately were still. The glare from the landing field was gone. The lighted lane through the jungle was dark again. Huyghens ushered the man from the space-boat up into his living quarters. There was a rustling stir, and Semper took his head from under his wing. He stared coldly at the two humans, spread monstrous, seven-foot wings, and fluttered them. He opened his beak and closed it with a snap.

"That's Semper," said Huyghens. "Semper Tyrannis. He's the rest of the terrestrial population here. Not being a fly-by-night sort of creature, he didn't come out to welcome you."

Bordman blinked at the huge bird, perched on a three-inch thick perch set in the wall.

"An eagle?" he demanded. "Kodiak bears — mutated ones, but still bears? — and now an eagle? You've a very nice fighting unit in the bears —"

"They're pack animals too," said Huyghens. "They can carry some hundreds of pounds without losing too much combat efficiency. And there's no problem of supply. They live off the jungle. Not sphexes, though. Nothing will eat a sphex."

He brought out glasses and a bottle and indicated a chair. Bordman put down his traveling bag, took a glass, and sat down.

"I'm curious," he observed. "Why Semper Tyrannis? I can understand Sitka Pete and Sourdough Charley as fighters. But why Semper?"

"He was bred for hawking," said Huyghens. "You sic a dog on something. You sic Semper Tyrannis. He's too big to ride on a hawking-glove, so the shoulders of my coat are padded to let him ride there. He's a flying scout. I've trained him to notify us of sphexes, and in flight he carried a tiny television camera. He's useful, but he hasn't the brains of the bears."

Bordman sat down and sipped at his glass.

"Interesting, very interesting! — Didn't you say something about shooting me?"

"I'm trying to think of a way out," Huyghens said. "Add up all the penalties for illegal colonization and I'd be in a very bad fix if you got away and reported this set-up. Shooting you would be logical."

"I see that," said Bordman reasonably. "But since the point has come up — I have a blaster trained on you from my pocket."

Huyghens shrugged.

"It's rather likely that my human confederates will be back here before your friends. You'd be in a very tight fix if my friends came back and found you more or less sitting on my corpse."

Bordman nodded.

"That's true. too. Also it's probable that your fellow-terrestrials wouldn't cooperate with me as they have with you. You seem to have the whip hand, even with my blaster trained on you. On the other hand, you could have killed me quite easily after the boat left, when I'd first landed. I'd have been quite unsuspicious. Therefore you may not really intend to murder me."

Huyghens shrugged again.

"So," said Bordman, "since the secret of getting along with people is that of postponing quarrels, suppose we postpone the question of who kills whom? Frankly, I'm going to send you to prison if I can. Unlawful colonization is very bad business. But I suppose you feel that you have to do something permanent about me. In your place I probably should, too. Shall we declare a truce?"

Huyghens indicated indifference.

"Then I do," Bordman said. "I have to! So —"

He pulled his hand out of his pocket and put a pocket blaster on the table. He leaned back.

"Keep it," said Huyghens. "Loren Two isn't a place where you live long unarmed." He turned to a cupboard. "Hungry?"

"I could eat," admitted Bordman.

Huyghens pulled out two meal-packs from the cupboard and inserted them in the readier below. He set out plates.

"Now, what happened to the official, licensed, authorized colony here?" asked Bordman briskly. "License issued eighteen months ago. There was a landing of colonists with a drone fleet of equipment and supplies. There've been four ship-contacts since. There should be several thousand robots being industrious under adequate human supervision. There should be a hundred-mile-square clearing, planted with food-plants for later human arrivals. There should be a landing-grid at least half-finished. Obviously there should be a space-beacon to guide ships to a landing. There isn't. There's no clearing visible from space. That Crete Line ship has been in orbit for three days, trying to find a place to drop me. Her skipper was fuming. Your beacon is the only one on the planet, and we found it by accident. What happened?"

Huyghens served the food. He said dryly:

"There could be a hundred colonies on this planet without any one knowing of any other. I can only guess about your robots, but I suspect they ran into sphexes."

Bordman paused, with his fork in his hand.

"I read up on this planet, since I was to report on its colony. A sphex is part of the inimical animal life here. Cold-blooded belligerent carnivore, not a lizard but a genus all its own. Hunts in packs. Seven to eight hundred pounds, when adult. Lethally dangerous and simply too numerous to fight. They're why no license was ever granted to human colonists. Only robots could work here, because they're machines. What animal attacks machines?"

Huyghens said:

"What machine attacks animals? The sphexes wouldn't bother robots, of course, but would robots bother the sphexes?"

Bordman chewed and swallowed.

"Hold it! I'll agree that you can't make a hunting-robot. A machine can discriminate, but it can't decide. That's why there's no danger of a robot revolt. They can't decide to do something for which they have no instructions. But this colony was planned with full knowledge of what robots can and can't do. As ground was cleared, it was enclosed in an electrified fence with no sphex could touch without frying."

Huyghens thoughtfully cut his food. After a moment:

"The landing was in the winter time," he observed. "It must have been, because the colony survived a while. And at a guess the last ship-landing was before the thaw. The years are eighteen months long here, you know."

"It was in winter that the landing was made," Bordman admitted. "And the last ship-landing was before spring. The idea was to get mines in operation for material, and to have ground cleared and enclosed in sphex-proof fence before the sphexes came back from the tropics. They winter there, I understand."

"Did you ever see a sphex?" asked Huyghens. Then he said, "No, of course not. But if you took a spitting cobra and crossed it with a wild-cat, painted it tan-and-blue and then gave it hydrophobia and homicidal mania at once, you might have one sphex. But not the race of sphexes. They can climb trees, by the way. A fence wouldn't stop them."

"An electrified fence," said Bordman. "Nothing could climb that!"

"Not one animal," Huyghens told him. "But sphexes are a race. The smell of one dead sphex brings others running with blood in their eyes. Leave a dead sphex alone for six hours and you've got them around by dozens. Two days and there are hundreds. Longer, and you've got thousands of them! They gather to caterwaul over their dead pal and hunt for whoever or whatever killed him."

He returned to his meal. A moment later he said:

"No need to wonder what happened to your colony. During the winter the robots burned out a clearing and put up an electrified fence according to the book. Come spring, the sphexes came back. They're curious, among their other madnesses. A sphex would try to climb the fence just to see what was behind it. He'd be electrocuted. His carcass would bring others, raging because a sphex was dead. Some of them would try to climb the fence, and die. And their corpses would bring others. Presently the fence would break down from the bodies hanging on it, or a bridge of dead beasts' carcasses would be built across it — and from as far downwind as the scent carried there'd be loping, raging, scent-crazed sphexes racing to the spot. They'd pour into the clearing through or over the fence, squalling and screeching for something to kill. I think they'd find it."

Bordman ceased to eat. He looked sick.

"There were pictures of sphexes in the data I read. I suppose that would account for — everything."

He tried to lift his fork. He put it down again.

"I can't eat," he said abruptly.

Huyghens made no comment. He finished his own meal, scowling. He rose and put the plates into the top of the cleaner.

"Let me see those reports, eh?" he asked dourly. "I'd like to see what sort of set-up they had, those robots."

Bordman hesitated and then opened the traveling bag. There was a micro-viewer and reels of film. One entire reel was labeled "Specifications for Construction, Colonial Survey," which would contain detailed plans and all requirements of material and workmanship for everything from desks, office, administrative personnel, for use of, to landing-grids, heavy-gravity planets, lift-capacity 100,000 Earth-tons. But Huyghens found another. He inserted it and spun the control swiftly here and there, pausing only briefly at index-frames until he came to the section he wanted. He began to study the information with growing impatience.

"Robots, robots, robots!" he snapped. "Why don't they leave them where they belong — in cities to do the dirty work, and on airless planets where nothing unexpected ever happens! Robots don't belong in new colonies. Your colonists depended on them for defense! Dammit, let a man work with robots long enough and he thinks all nature is as limited as they are! This is a plan to set up a controlled environment — on Loren Two! Controlled environment —" He swore. "Complacent, idiotic, desk-bound half-wits!"

"Robots are all right," said Bordman. "We couldn't run civilization without them."

"But you can't tame a wilderness with 'em," snapped Huyghens. "You had a dozen men landed, with fifty assembled robots to start with. There were parts for fifteen hundred more, and I'll bet anything I've got the ship-contacts landed more still!"

"They did," admitted Bordman.

"I despise 'em," growled Huyghens. "I feel about 'em the way the old Greeks felt about slaves. They're for menial work — the sort of work a man will perform for himself, but that he won't do for another man for pay. Degrading work!"

"Quite aristocratic!" said Bordman with a touch of irony. "I take it that robots clean out the bear-quarters downstairs."

"No!" snapped Huyghens. "I do. They're my friends. They fight for me. No robot would do the job right!"

He growled, again. The noises of the night went on outside. Organ-tones and hiccoughings and the sound of tack-hammers and slamming doors. Somewhere there was a singularly exact replica of the discordant squeakings of a rusty pump.

"I'm looking," said Huyghens at the micro-viewer, "for the record of their mining operations. An open-pit operation would not mean a thing. But if they had driven a tunnel, and somebody was there supervising the robots when the colony was wiped out, there's an off-chance he survived a while."

Bordman regarded him with suddenly intent eyes.

"And —"

"Dammit," snapped Huyghens, "if so I'll go see! He'd — they'd have no chance at all, otherwise. Not that the chance is good in any case."

Bordman raised his eyebrows.

"I've told you I'll send you to prison if I can," he said. "You've risked the lives of millions of people, maintaining non-quarantined communication with an unlicensed planet. If you did rescue somebody from the ruins of the robot colony — does it occur to you that they'd be witnesses to your unauthorized presence here?"

Huyghens spun the viewer again. He stopped, switched back and forth, and found what he wanted. He muttered in satisfaction: "They did run a tunnel!" Aloud he said, "I'll worry about witnesses when I have to."

He pushed aside another cupboard door. Inside it were the odds and ends a man makes use of to repair the things about his house that he never notices until they go wrong. There was an assortment of wires, transistors, bolts, and similar stray items.

"What now?" asked Bordman mildly.

"I'm going to try to find out if there's anybody left alive over there. I'd have checked before, if I'd known the colony existed. I can't prove they're all dead, but I may prove that somebody's still alive. It's barely two weeks' journey away from here. Odd that two colonies picked spots so near!"

He picked over the oddments he'd selected.

"Confound it!" Bordman said. "How can you check if somebody's alive some hundreds of miles away?"

Huyghens threw a switch and took down the wall-panel, exposing electronic apparatus and circuits behind. He busied himself with it.

"Ever think about hunting for a castaway?" he asked over his shoulder. "Here's a planet with some tens of millions of square miles on it. You know there's a ship down. You've no idea where. You assume the survivors have power — no civilized man will be without power very long, so long as he can smelt metals! — but making a space-beacon calls for high-precision measurements and workmanship. It's not to be improvised. So what will your shipwrecked civilized man do, to guide a rescue-ship to one or two square miles he occupies among some tens of millions on the planet?"

"What?"

"He's had to go primitive, to begin with," Huyghens explained. "He cooks his meals over a fire, and so on. He has to make a strictly primitive signal. It's all he can do without gauges and micrometers and special tools. But he can fill all the planet's atmosphere with a signal that searches for him can't miss. You see?"

Bordman thought irritably. He shook his head.

"He'll make," said Huyghens, "a spark transmitter. He'll fix its output at the shortest frequency he can contrive, somewhere in the five-to-fifty-meter waveband, but it will be tuned very broad — and it will be a plainly human signal. He'll start it broadcasting. Some of those frequencies will go all around the planet under the ionosphere. Any ship that comes in under the radio roof will pick up his signal, get a fix on it, move and get another fix, and then go straight to where the castaway is waiting placidly in a hand-braided hammock, sipping whatever sort of drink he's improvised out of the local vegetation."

Bordman said grudgingly:

"Now that you mention it, of course. . . ."

"My space-phone picks up microwaves," said Huyghens. "I'm shifting a few elements to make it listen for longer stuff. It won't be efficient, but it will catch a distress-signal if one's in the air. I don't expect it, though."

He worked. Bordman sat still a long time, watching him. Down below, a rhythmic sort of sound arose. It was Sourdough Charley, snoring.

Sitka Pete grunted in his sleep. He was dreaming. In the general room of the station Semper blinked his eyes rapidly and then tucked his head under a gigantic wing and went to sleep. The noises of Loren Two jungle came through the steel-shuttered windows. The nearer moon — which had passed overhead not long before the ringing of the alarm-bell — again came soaring over the eastern horizon. It sped across the sky.

Inside the station, Bordman said angrily:

"See here, Huyghens! You've reason to kill me. Apparently you don't intend to. You've excellent reason to leave that robot colony strictly alone. But you're preparing to help, if there's anybody alive to need it. And yet you're a criminal, and I mean a criminal! There've been some ghastly bacteria exported from planets like Loren Two. There've been plenty of lives lost in consequence, and you're risking more. Why the hell do you do it? Why do you do something that could produce monstrous results to other human beings?"

Huyghens grunted.

"You're assuming there are no sanitary and quarantine precautions taken by my partners. As a matter of fact, there are. They're taken, all right! As for the rest, you wouldn't understand."

"I don't understand," snapped Bordman, "but that's no proof I can't. Why are you a criminal?"

Huyghens painstakingly used a screwdriver inside the wall-panel. He lifted out a small electronic assembly, and began to fit in a spaghettied new assembly with larger units.

"I'm cutting my amplification here to hell-and-gone," he observed, "but I think it'll do . . . I'm doing what I'm doing," he added calmly, "because it seems to me it fits what I think I am. Everybody acts according to his own real notion of himself. You're a conscientious citizen, a loyal official, a well-adjusted personality. You act that way. You consider yourself an intelligent rational animal. But you don't act that way! You're reminding me of my need to shoot you or something similar, which a merely rational animal would try to make me forget. You happen, Bordman, to be a man. So am I. But I'm aware of it. Therefore, I deliberately do things a merely rational animal wouldn't, because they're my notion of what a man who's more than a rational animal should do."

He tightened one small screw after another.

Bordman said:

"Oh. Religion."

"Self-respect," corrected Huyghens. "I don't like robots. They're too much like rational animals. A robot will do whatever it can that its supervisor requires it to do. A merely rational animal will do whatever circumstances require it to do. I wouldn't like a robot unless it had some idea of what was fitting and would spit in my eye if I tried to make it do something else. The bears downstairs, now. . . . They're no robots! They are loyal and honorable beasts, but they'd turn and tear me to bits if I tried to make them do something against their natures. Faro Nell would fight me and all creation together, if I tried to harm Nugget. It would be unintelligent and unreasonable and irrational. She'd lose out and get killed. But I like her that way! And I'll fight you and all creation when you make me try to do something against my nature.

I'll be stupid and unreasonable and irrational about it." Then he grinned over his shoulder. "So will you. Only you don't realize it."

He turned back to his task. After a moment he fitted the manual-control knob over a shaft in his haywire assembly.

"What did somebody try to make you do?" asked Bordman shrewdly. "What was demanded of you that turned you into a criminal? What are you in revolt against?"

Huyghens threw a switch. He began to turn the knob which controlled the knob of his makeshift receiver.

"Why," he said, "when I was young the people around me tried to make me into a conscientious citizen and a loyal employee and a well-adjusted personality. They tried to make me into a highly intelligent rational animal and nothing more. The difference between us, Bordman, is that I found it out. Naturally, I rev —"

He stopped short. Faint, crackling, frying sounds came from the speaker of the space-phone now modified to receive what once were called short waves.

Huyghens listened. He cocked his head intently. He turned the knob very, very slowly. Bordman made an arrested gesture, to call attention to something in the sibilant sound. Huyghens nodded. He turned the knob again, with infinitesimal increments.

Out of the background noise came a patterned mutter. As Huyghens shifted the tuning, it grew louder. It reached a volume where it was unmistakable. It was a sequence of sounds like a discordant buzzing. There were three half-second buzzings with half-second pauses between. Another two-second pause and three half-second pauses between. Another two-second pause and three half-second buzzings, again. Then silence for five seconds. Then the pattern repeated.

"The devil!" said Huyghens. "That's a human signal! Mechanically made, too. In fact, it used to be a standard distress call. It was termed an SOS. Though I've no idea what that meant. Anyhow, somebody must have read old-fashioned novels some time, to know about it. And so someone is still alive over at your licensed but now smashed-up robot colony. And they're asking for help. I'd say they're likely to need it."

He looked at Bordman.

"The intelligent thing to do is sit back and wait for a ship, either my friends' or yours. A ship can help survivors or castaways much better than we can. It could even find them more easily. But maybe time is important to the poor devils. So I'm going to take the bears and see if I can reach them. You can wait here, if you like. What say?"

Bordman snapped angrily.

"Don't be a fool! Of course I'm coming! What do you take me for? And two of us should have four times the chance as one!"

Huyghens grinned.

"Not quite. You forget Sitka Pete and Sourdough Charley and Faro Nell. There'll be five of us if you come, instead of four. And, of course, Nugget has to come — and he'll be no help — but Semper may make up for him. You won't quadruple our chances, Bordman, but I'll be glad to have you if you want to be stupid and unreasonable and not at all rational, and come with me."

There was a jagged spur of stone looming precipitously over a river-valley. A thousand feet below, a broad stream ran westward to the sea. Twenty miles to the east, a wall of mountains rose sheer against the sky, its peaks seeming to blend to a remarkable evenness of height. Rolling, tumbled ground lay between for as far as the eye could see.

A speck in the sky came swiftly downward. Great pinions spread and flapped, and icy eyes surveyed the rocky space. With more flappings, Semper the eagle came to ground. He folded his huge wings and turned his head jerkily, his eyes unblinking. A tiny harness held a miniature camera against his chest. He strutted over to the bare stone to the highest point and stood there, a lonely and arrogant figure in the vastness.

Crashings and rustlings, and snuffling sounds, and Sitka Pete came lumbering out into the clear space. He wore a harness too, and a pack. The harness was complex, because it had to hold a pack not only in normal travel, but when he stood on his hind legs, and it must not hamper the use of his forepaws in combat.

He went cagily over the open area. He peered over the edge of the spur's farthest tip, and prowled to the other side and looked down. Once he moved close to Semper and the eagle opened his great curved beak and uttered an indignant noise. Sitka paid no attention.

He relaxed, satisfied. He sat down untidily, his hind legs sprawling. He wore an air approaching benevolence as he surveyed the landscape about and below him.

More snufflings and crashings. Sourdough Charley came into view with Huyghens and Bordman behind him. Sourdough carried a pack, too. Then there was a squealing and Nugget scurried up from the rear, impelled by a whack from his mother. Faro Nell appeared, with the carcass of a stag-like animal lashed to her harness.

"I picked this place from a space-photo," said Huyghens, "to make a directional fix for you. I'll get set up."

He swung his pack from his shoulder to the ground, and extracted an obviously self-constructed device which he set on the ground. It had a whip aerial, which he extended. Then he plugged in a considerable length of flexible wire and unfolded a tiny, improvised directional aerial with an even tinier booster at its base. Bordman slipped his pack from his shoulders and watched. Huyghens put a pair of head-phones over his ears. He looked up and said sharply:

"Watch the bears, Bordman. The wind's blowing up the way we came. Anything that trails us will send its scent on before. The bears will tell us."

He busied himself with the instruments he'd brought. He heard the hissing, frying, background noise which could be anything at all except a human signal. He reached out and swung the small aerial around. Rasping, buzzing tones came in, faintly and then loudly. This receiver, though, had been made for this particular wave-band. It was much more efficient than the modified space-phone had been. It picked up three short buzzes, three long ones, and three short ones again. Three dots, three dashes, and three dots. Over and over again. S-O-S. S-O-S. S-O-S.

Huyghens took a reading and moved the directional aerial a carefully measured distance. He took another reading, shifted it yet again and again, carefully marking and measuring each spot and taking notes of the instrument readings. When he finished, he had checked the direction of the signal not only by loudness but by phase, and had as accurate a fix as could possibly be made with portable apparatus.

Sourdough growled softly. Sitka Pete whiffed the air and arose from his sitting position. Faro Nell whacked Nugget, sending him whimpering to the farthest corner of the flat plane. She stood bristling, facing downhill the way they'd come.

"Damn!" said Huyghens.

He got up and waved his arm at Semper, who had turned his head at the stirrings. Semper squawked and dived off the spur, and was immediately fighting the down-draught beyond it. As Huyghens reached his weapon, the eagle came back overhead. He went magnificently past, a hundred feet high, careening and flapping in the tricky currents. He screamed, abruptly, and screamed again. Huyghens swung a tiny vision-plate from its strap to where he could look into it. He saw, of course, what the tiny camera on Semper's chest could see — reeling, swaying terrain as Semper saw it, though of course without his breadth of field. There were moving objects to be seen through the shifting trees. Their coloring was unmistakable.

"Sphexes," said Huyghens dourly. "Eight of them. Don't look for them to follow our tracks, Bordman. They run parallel to a trail on either side. That way they attack in breadth and all at once they catch up. And listen! The bears can handle anything they tangle with — it's our job to pick off the loose ones. And aim for the body! The bullets explode."

He threw off the safety of his weapon. Faro Nell, uttering thunderous growls, went padding to a place between Sitka Pete and Sourdough. Sitka glanced at her and made a whuffing noise, as if derisive of her bloodcurdling sounds. Sourdough grunted. He and Sitka moved farther away from Nell to either side. They would cover the wider front.

There was no other sign of life than the shrillings of the incredible tiny creatures which on this planet were birds, and Faro Nell's deep-bass, raging growls, and then the click of Bordman's safety going off as he got ready to use the weapon Huyghens had given him.

Semper screamed again, flapping low above the tree-tops, following parti-colored, monstrous shapes beneath.

Eight blue-and-tan fiends came racing out of the underbrush. They had spiny fringes, and horns, and glaring eyes, and they looked as if they had come straight out of hell. On the instant of their appearance they leaped, emitting squalling, spitting squeals that were like the cries of fighting tom-cats ten thousand times magnified. Huyghens' rifle cracked, and its sound was wiped out in the louder detonation of its bullet in sphexian flesh. A tan-and-blue monster tumbled over, shrieking. Bordman fired, and his bullet exploded against a tree. Sitka Pete brought his massive forepaws in a clapping, monstrous ear-boxing motion. A sphex died.

Then Bordman fired again. Sourdough Charley whuffed. He fell forward upon a spitting, bi-colored fiend, rolled him over, and raked with his hind-claws. The belly-hide of the sphex was tenderer than the rest. The creature rolled away, snapping at its own wounds. Another sphex found itself shaken loose from the tumult about Sitka Pete. It whirled to leap on him from behind, and Huyghens fired. Two plunged upon Faro Nell, and Bordman blasted one and Faro Nell disposed of the other in awesome fury.

Then Sitka Pete heaved himself erect — seeming to drip sphexes — and Sourdough waddled over and pulled one off and killed it and went back for another. . . . Then both rifles cracked together and there was suddenly nothing left to fight.

The bear prowled from one to another of the corpses. Sitka Pete rumbled and lifted up a limp head. Crash! Then another. He went over the lot, whether or not they showed signs of life. When he had finished, they were wholly still.

Semper came flapping down out of the sky. He had screamed and fluttered overhead as the fight went on. Now he landed with a rush. Huyghens went soothingly from one bear to another, calming them with his voice. It took longest to calm Faro Nell, licking Nugget with impassioned solicitude and growling horribly as she licked.

"Come along now," said Huyghens, when Sitka showed signs of intending to sit down again. "Heave these carcasses over a cliff. Come along! Sitka! Sourdough! Hup!"

He guided them as the two big males somewhat fastidiously lifted up the nightmarish creatures and carried them to the edge of the spur of stone. They let the beasts go bouncing and sliding down into the valley.

"That," said Huyghens, "is so their pals will gather round them and caterwaul their woes where there's no trail of ours to give them ideas. If we'd been near a river I'd have dumped them in to float downstream and gather mourners wherever they stranded. Around the station I incinerate them. If I had to leave them, I'd make tracks away. About fifty miles upwind would be a good idea."

He opened the pack Sourdough carried and extracted giant-sized swabs and some gallons of antiseptic. He tended the three Kodiaks in turn, swabbing not only the cuts and scratches they'd received, but deeply soaking their fur where there could be suspicion of spilled sphex-blood.

"This antiseptic deodorizes, too," he told Bordman. "Or we'd be trailed by any sphex who passed leeward of us. When we start off, I'll swab the bears' paws for the same reason."

Bordman was very quiet. He'd missed his first shot, but the last few seconds of the fight he'd fired very deliberately and every bullet hit. Now he said bitterly:

"If you're instructing me so I can carry on should you be killed, I doubt that it's worthwhile!"

Huyghens felt in his pack and unfolded the enlargement he'd made of the space-photos of this part of the planet. He carefully oriented the map with distant landmarks, and drew a line across the photo.

"The SOS signal comes from somewhere close to the robot colony," he reported. "I think a little to the south of it. Probably from a mine they'd opened up, on the far side of the Sere Plateau. See how I've marked this map? Two fixes, one from the station and the other from here. I came away off-course to get a fix here so we'd have two position-lines to the transmitter. The signal could have come from the other side of the planet. But it doesn't."

"The odds would be astronomical against other castaways," protested Bordman.

"No," said Huyghens. "Ships have been coming here. To the robot-colony. One could have crashed. And I have friends, too."

He repacked his apparatus and gestured to the bears. He led them beyond the scene of combat and carefully swabbed off their paws, so they could not possibly leave a train of sphex-blood scent behind them. He waved Semper, the eagle, aloft.

"Let's go," he told the Kodiaks. "Yonder! Hup!"

The party headed downhill and into the jungle again. Now it was Sourdough's turn to take the lead, and Sitka Pete prowled more widely behind him. Faro Nell trailed the men, with Nugget. She kept a sharp eye upon the cub. He was a baby, still; he only weighed six hundred pounds. And of course she watched against danger from the rear.

Overhead, Semper fluttered and flew in giant circles and spirals, never going very far away. Huyghens referred constantly to the screen which showed what the air-borne camera saw. The image tilted and circled and banked and swayed. It was by no means the best air-reconnaissance that could be imagined, but it was the best that would work. Presently Huyghens said:

"We swing to the right, here. The going's bad straight ahead, and it looks like a pack of sphexes has killed and is feeding."

Bordman said:

"It's against reason for carnivores to be as thick as you say! There has to be a certain amount of other animal life for every meat-eating beast. Too many of them would eat all the game and starve."

"They're gone all winter," explained Huyghens, "which around here isn't as severe as you might think. And a good many animals seem to breed just after the sphexes go south. Also, the sphexes aren't around all the warm weather. There's a sort of peak, and then for a matter of weeks you won't see one of them, and suddenly the jungle swarms with them again. Then, presently, they head south. Apparently they're migratory in some fashion, but nobody knows." He said dryly. "There haven't been many naturalists around on this planet. The animal life's inimical."

Bordman fretted. He was accustomed to arrival at a partly or completely finished colonial set-up, and to pass upon the completion or non-completion of the installation as designed. Now he was in an intolerably hostile environment, depending upon an illegal colonist for his life, engaged upon a demoralizingly indefinite enterprise — because the mechanical spark-signal could be working long after its constructors were dead — and his ideas about a number of matters were shaken. He was alive, for example, because of three giant Kodiak bears and a bald eagle. He and Huyghens could have been surrounded by ten thousand robots, and they'd have been killed. Sphexes and robots would have ignored each other, and sphexes would have made straight for the men, who'd have had less than four seconds in which to discover for themselves that they were attacked, prepare to defend themselves, and kill the eight sphexes.

Bordman's convictions as a civilized man were shaken. Robots were marvelous contrivances for doing the expected, accomplishing the planned, coping with the predicted. But they also had defects. Robots could only follow instructions. If this thing happens, do this, if that thing happens, do that. But before something else, neither this or that, robots were helpless. So a robot civilization worked only in an environment where nothing unanticipated ever turned up, and human supervisors never demanded anything unexpected. Bordman was appalled.

He found Nugget, the cub, ambling uneasily in his wake. The cub flattened his ears miserably when Bordman glanced at him. It occurred to the man that Nugget was receiving a lot of disciplinary thumpings from Faro Nell. He was knocked about psychologically. His lack of information and unfitness for independent survival in this environment was being hammered into him.

"Hi, Nugget," said Bordman ruefully. "I feel just about the way you do!"

Nugget brightened visibly. He frisked. He tended to gambol. He looked hopefully up into Bordman's face.

The man reached out and patted Nugget's head. It was the first time in his life that he'd ever petted an animal.

He heard a snuffling sound behind him. Skin crawled at the back of his neck. He whirled.

Faro Nell regarded him — eighteen hundred pounds of she-bear only ten feet away and looking into his eyes. For one panicky moment Bordman went cold all over. Then he realized that Faro Nell's eyes were not burning. She was not snarling, nor did she emit those blood-curdling sounds which the bare prospect of danger to Nugget had produced up on the rocky spur. She looked at him blandly. In fact, after a moment she swung off on some independent investigation of a matter that had aroused her curiosity.

The traveling-party went on, Nugget frisking beside Bordman and tending to bump into him out of pure cub-clumsiness. Now and again he looked adoringly at Bordman, in the instant and overwhelming affection of the very young.

Bordman trudged on. Presently he glanced behind again. Faro Nell was now ranging more widely. She was well satisfied to have Nugget in the immediate care of a man. From time to time he got on her nerves.

A little while later Bordman called ahead.

"Huyghens! Look here! I've been appointed nursemaid to Nugget!"

Huyghens looked back.

"Oh, slap him a few times and he'll go back to his mother."

"The devil I will!" said Bordman. "I like it!"

The traveling-party went on.

When night fell, they camped. There could be no fire, of course, because all the minute night-things about would come to dance in the glow. But there could not be darkness, equally, because night-walkers hunted in the dark. So Huyghens set out barrier-lamps which made a wall of twilight around their halting-place, and the stag-like creature Faro Nell had carried became their evening meal. Then they slept — at least the men did — and the bears dozed and snorted and waked and dozed again. Semper sat immobile with his head under his wing on a tree limb. Presently there was a glorious cool hush and all the world glowed in morning-light diffused through the jungle by a newly risen sun. Then they arose and pushed on.

This day they stopped stock-still for two hours while sphexes puzzled over the trail the bears had left. Huyghens discoursed on the need of an anti-scent, to be used on the boots of men and the paws of bears, which would make the following of their trails unpopular with sphexes. Bordman seized upon the idea and suggested that a sphex-repellent odor might be worked out, which would make a human revolting to a sphex. If that were done, humans could go freely about, unmolested.

"Like stink-bugs," said Huyghens, sardonically. "A very intelligent idea! Very rational! You can feel proud!"

And suddenly Bordman was not proud of the idea at all.

They camped again. On the third night they were at the base of that remarkable formation, the Sere Plateau, which from a distance looked like a mountain range but was actually a desert tableland. It was not reasonable for a desert to be raised high, while lowlands had rain, but on the fourth morning they found out why. They saw, far, far away, a truly monstrous mountain-mass at the end of the long expanse of the plateau. It was like the prow of a ship. It lay, so Huyghens observed, directly in line with the prevailing winds, and divided them as a ship's prow divides the waters. The moisture-bearing air-currents flowed beside the plateau, not over it, and its interior was desert in the unscreened sunshine of the high altitudes.

It took them a full day to get halfway up the slope. And here, twice, as they climbed, Semper flew screaming over aggregations of sphexes to one side of them or the other. These were much larger groups than Huyghens had ever seen before, fifty to a hundred monstrosities together, where a dozen was a large hunting-pack elsewhere. He looked in the screen which showed him what Semper saw, four to five miles away. The sphexes padded uphill toward the Sere Plateau in a long line. Fifty — sixty — seventy tan-and-azure beasts out of hell.

"I'd hate to have that bunch jump us," he said candidly to Bordman. "I don't think we'd stand a chance."

"Here's where a robot tank would be useful," Bordman observed.

"Anything armored," conceded Huyghens. "One man in an armored station like mine would be safe. But if he killed a sphex he'd be besieged. He'd have to stay holed up, breathing the smell of the dead sphex, until the odor'd gone away. And he mustn't kill any others or he'd be besieged until winter came."

Bordman did not suggest the advantages of robots in other directions. At that moment, for example, they were working their way up a slope which averaged fifty degrees. The bears climbed without effort despite their burdens. For the men it was infinite toil. Semper, the eagle, manifested impatience with bears and men alike, who crawled so slowly up an incline over which he soared.

He went ahead up the mountainside and teetered in the air-currents at the plateau's edge. Huyghens looked in the vision-plate by which he reported.

"How the devil," panted Bordman, panting — they had

stopped for a breather, and the bears waited patiently for them — "how do you train bears like this? I can understand Semper."

"I don't train them," said Huyghens, staring into the plate. "They're mutations. In heredity the sex-linkage of physical characteristics is standard stuff. There's also been some sound work done on the gene-linkage of psychological factors. There was need, on my home planet, for an animal who could fight like a fiend, live off the land, carry a pack and get along with men at least as well as dogs do. In the old days they'd have tried to breed the desired physical properties in an animal who already had the personality they wanted. Something like a giant dog, say. But back home they went at it the other way about. They picked the wanted physical characteristics and bred for the personality, the psychology. The job got done over a century ago. The Kodiak bear named Kodius Champion was the first real success. He had everything that was wanted. These bears are his descendants."

"They look normal," commented Bordman.

"They are!" said Huyghens warmly. "Just as normal as an honest dog! They're not trained, like Semper. They train themselves! He looked back into the plate in his hands, which showed the ground six or seven thousand feet higher. "Semper, now, is a trained bird without too much brain. He's educated — a glorified hawk. But the bears want to get along with men. They're emotionally dependent on us. Like dogs. Semper's a servant, but they're companions and friends. He's trained, but they're loyal. He's conditioned. They love us. He'd abandon me if he ever realized he could; he thinks he can only eat what men feed him. But the bears wouldn't want to. They like us. I admit I like them. Maybe because they like me."

Bordman said deliberately:

"Aren't you a trifle loose-tongued, Huyghens? You've told me something that will locate and convict the people who set you up here. It shouldn't be hard to find where bears were bred for psychological mutations. I can find out where you came from now, Huyghens!"

Huyghens looked up from the plate with its tiny swaying television image.

"No harm done," he said amiably. "I'm a criminal there, too. It's officially on record that I kidnapped these bears and escaped with them. Which, on my home planet, is about as heinous a crime as a man can commit. It's worse than horse-theft back on Earth in the old days. The kin and cousin of my bears are highly thought of. I'm quite a criminal, back home."

Bordman stared.

"Did you steal them?" he demanded.

"Confidentially," said Huyghens. "No. But prove it!" Then he said: "Take a look in this plate. See what Semper can see up at the plateau's edge."

Bordman squinted aloft, where the eagle flew in great sweeps and dashes. Somehow, by the experience of the past few days, Bordman knew that Semper was screaming fiercely as he flew. He made a dart toward the plateau's border.

Bordman looked at the transmitter picture. It was only four inches by six, but it was perfectly without grain and accurate in color. It moved and turned as the camera-bearing eagle swooped and circled. For an instant the screen showed the steeply sloping mountainside, and off at one edge the party of men and bears could be seen as dots. Then it swept away and showed the top of the plateau.

There were sphexes. A pack of two hundred trotted toward the desert interior. They moved at leisure, in the open. The viewing camera reeled, and there were more. As Bordman watched and as the bird flew higher, he could see still other sphexes moving up over the edge of the plateau from a small erosion-defile here and another one there. The Sere Plateau was alive with the hellish creatures. It was inconceivable that there should be game enough for them to live on. They were visible as herds of cattle would be visible on grazing planets.

It was simply impossible.

"Migrating," observed Huyghens. "I said they did. They're headed somewhere. Do you know, I doubt that it would be healthy for us to try to cross the Plateau through such a swarm of sphexes!"

Bordman swore, in abrupt change of mood.

"But the signal's still coming through. Somebody's alive over at the robot colony. Must we wait till the migration's over?"

"We don't know," Huyghens pointed out, "that they'll stay alive. They may need help badly. We have to get to them. But at the same time —"

He glanced at Sourdough Charley and Sitka Pete, clinging patiently to the mountainside while the men rested and talked. Sitka had managed to find a place to sit down, one massive paw anchoring him in place.

Huyghens waved his arms, pointing in a new direction.

"Let's go!" he called briskly. "Let's go! Yonder! Hup!"

They followed the slopes of Sere Plateau, neither ascending to its level top — where the sphexes congregated — nor descending into the foothills where sphexes assembled. They moved along hillsides and mountain-flanks which sloped anywhere from thirty to sixty degrees, and they did not cover much territory. They practically forgot what it was to walk on level ground.

At the end of the sixth day, they camped on top of a massive boulder which projected from a mountainous stony wall. There was barely enough room on the boulder for all the party. Faro Nell fussily insisted that Nugget should be in the safest part, which meant near the mountain-flank. She would have crowded the men outward, but Nugget whimpered for Bordman. Wherefore, when Bordman moved to comfort him, Faro Nell drew back and snorted at Sitka and Sourdough and they made room for her near the edge.

It was a hungry camp. They had come upon tiny rills upon occasion, flowing down the mountainside. Here the bears had drunk deeply and the men had filled canteens. But this was the third night on the mountainside, and there had been no game at all. Huyghens made no move to bring out food for Bordman or himself. Bordman made no comment. He was beginning to participate in the relationship between bears and men, which was not the slavery of the bears but something more. It was two-way. He felt it.

"You'd think," he said, "that since the sphexes don't seem to hunt on their way uphill, there should be some game. They ignore everything as they file up."

This was true enough. The normal fighting formation of sphexes was line abreast, which automatically surrounded anything which offered to flee and outflanked anything which offered fight. But here they ascended the mountain in long files, one after the other, apparently following long-established trails. The wind blew along the slopes and carried scent sideways. But the sphexes were not diverted from their chosen paths. The long processions of hideous blue-and-tawny creatures — it was hard to think of them as natural beasts, male and female and laying eggs like reptiles on other planets — the long processions simply climbed.

"There've been other thousands of beasts before them," said Huyghens. "They must have been crowding this way for days or even weeks. We've seen tens of thousands in Semper's camera. They must be uncountable, altogether. The first-comers ate all the game there was, and the last-comers have something else on whatever they use for minds."

Bordman protested:

"But so many carnivores in one place is impossible! I know they are here, but they can't be!"

"They're cold-blooded," Huyghens pointed out. "They don't burn food to sustain body-temperature. After all, lots of creatures go for long periods without eating. Even bears hibernate. But this isn't hibernation — or estivation, either."

He was setting up the radiation-wave receiver in the darkness. There was no point of attempting a fix here. The transmitter was on the other side of the sphex-crowded Sere Plateau. The men and bears would commit suicide by crossing here.

Even so, Huyghens turned on the receiver. There came the whispering, scratchy sound of background-noise, and then the signal. Three dots, three dashes, three dots. Huyghens turned it off. Bordman said:

"Shouldn't we have answered that signal before we left the station? To encourage them?"

"I doubt they have a receiver," said Huyghens. "They won't expect an answer for months, anyhow. They'd hardly listen all the time, and if they're living in a mine-tunnel and trying to sneak out for food to stretch their supplies, they'll be too busy to try to make complicated records or relays."

Bordman was silent for a moment or two.

"We've got to get food for the bears," he said presently. "Nugget's weaned, and he's hungry."

"We will," Huyghens promised. "I may be wrong, but it seems to me that the number of sphexes climbing the mountain is less than yesterday and the day before. We may have just about crossed the path of their migration. They're thinning out. When we're past their trail, we'll have to look out for night-walkers and the like again. But I think they wiped out all animal life on their migration-route."

He was not quite right. He was waked in darkness by the sound of slapping and the grunting of bears. Feather-light puffs of breeze beat upon his face. He struck his belt-lamp sharply and the world was hidden by a whitish film which snatched itself away. Something flapped. Then he saw the stars and the emptiness on the edge of which they camped. Then big white things flapped toward him.

Sitka Pete whuffed mightily and swatted. Faro Nell grunted and swung. She caught something in her claws.

"Watch this!" said Huyghens.

More things strangely-shaped and pallid like human skin reeled and flapped crazily toward him.

A huge hairy paw reached up into the light-beam and snatched a flying thing out of it. Another great paw. The three great Kodiaks were on their hind legs, swatting at creatures which flittered insanely, unable to resist the fascination of the glaring lamp. Because of their wild gyrations it was impossible to see them in detail, but they were those unpleasant night-creatures which looked like plucked flying monkeys but were actually something quite different.

The bears did not snarl or snap. They swatted, with a remarkable air of business-like competence and purpose. Small mounds of broken things built up about their feet.

Suddenly there were no more. Huyghens snapped off the light. The bears crunched and fed busily in the darkness.

"Those things are carnivores *and* blood-suckers, Bordman," said Huyghens calmly. "They drain their victims of blood like vampire-bats — they've some trick of not waking them — and when they're dead the whole tribe eats. But bears have thick fur, and they wake when they're touched. And they're omnivorous. They'll eat anything but sphexes, and like it. You might say those night-creatures came to lunch. They *are* it, for the bears, who are living off the country as usual."

Bordman uttered a sudden exclamation. He made a tiny light, and blood flowed down his hand. Huyghens passed over his pocket kit of antiseptic and bandages. Bordman stanched the bleeding and bound up his hand. Then he realized that Nugget chewed on something. When he turned the light, Nugget swallowed convulsively. It appeared that he had caught and devoured the creature which had drawn blood from Bordman. But he'd lost none to speak of, at that.

In the morning they started along the sloping scarp of the plateau once more. After marching silently for awhile, Bordman said:

"Robots wouldn't have handled those vampire-things, Huyghens."

"Oh, they could be built to watch for them," said Huyghens, tolerantly. "But you'd have to swat for yourself. I prefer the bears."

He led the way on. Twice Huyghens halted to examine the ground about the mountains' bases through binoculars. He looked encouraged as they went on. The monstrous peak which was like the prow of a ship at the end of the Sere Plateau was visibly nearer. Toward midday, indeed, it loomed high above the horizon, no more than fifteen miles away. And at midday Huyghens called a final halt.

"No more congregations of sphexes down below," he said

cheerfully, "and we haven't seen a climbing line of them in miles." The crossing of sphex-trail had meant simply waiting until one party had passed, and then crossing before another came into view. "I've a hunch we've left their migration route behind. Let's see what Semper tells us!"

He waved the eagle aloft. Like all creatures other than men, the bird normally functioned only for the satisfaction of his appetite, and then tended to loaf or sleep. He had ridden the last few miles perched on Sitka Pete's pack. Now he soared upward and Huyghens watched in the small vision-plate.

Semper went soaring. The image on the plate swayed and turned, and in minutes was above the plateau's edge. Here there were some patches of brush and the ground rolled a little. But as Semper towered higher still, the inner desert appeared. Nearby, it was clear of beasts. Only once, when the eagle banked sharply and the camera looked along the long dimension of the plateau, did Huyghens see any sign of the blue-and-tan beasts. There he saw what looked like masses amounting to herds. Incredible, of course; carnivores do not gather in herds.

"We go straight up," said Huyghens with satisfaction. "We cross the Plateau here, and we can edge downwind a bit, even. I think we'll find something interesting on our way to your robot colony."

He waved to the bears to go ahead uphill.

They reached the top hours later, barely before sunset. And they saw game. Not much, but game at the grassy, brushy border of the desert. Huyghens brought down a shaggy ruminant which surely would not live on a desert. When night fell there was an abrupt chill in the air. It was much colder than night temperatures on the slopes. The air was thin. Bordman thought and presently guessed at the cause. In the lee of the prow-mountain the air was calm. There were no clouds. The ground radiated its heat to empty space. It could be bitterly cold in the night-time here.

"And hot by day," Huyghens agreed when he mentioned it. "The sunshine's terrifically hot where the air is thin, but on most mountains there's wind. By day, here, the ground will tend to heat up like the surface of a planet without atmosphere. It may be a hundred and forty or fifty degrees on the sand at midday. But it should be cold at night."

It was. Before midnight Huyghens built a fire. There could be no danger of night-walkers were the temperature dropped to freezing.

In the morning the men were stiff and cold, but the bears

snorted and moved about briskly. They seemed to revel in the morning chill. Sitka and Sourdough Charley, in fact, became festive and engaged in mock fight, whacking each other with blows that were only feigned, but would have crushed the skull of any man. Nugget sneezed with excitement as he watched them. Faro Nell regarded them with female disapproval.

They started on. Semper seemed sluggish. After a single brief flight he descended and rode on Sitka's pack, as on the previous day. He perched there, surveying the landscape as it changed from semi-arid to pure desert in their progress. He would not fly. Soaring birds do not like to fly when there are no winds to make currents of which they can take advantage.

Once Huyghens stopped and pointed out to Bordman exactly where they were on the enlarged photograph taken from space, and the exact spot from which the distress-signal seemed to come.

"You're doing it in case something happens to you," said Bordman. "I admit it's sense, but — what could I do to help those survivors even if I got to them, without you?"

"What you've learned about sphexes would help," said Huyghens. "The bears would help. And we left a note back at my station. Whoever grounds at the landing field back there — and the beacon's working — will find instructions to come to the place we're trying to reach."

They started walking again. The narrow patch of non-desert border of the Sere Plateau was behind them, now, and they marched across powdery desert sand.

"See here," said Bordman. "I want to know something. You tell me you're listed as a bear-thief on your home planet. You tell me it's a lie, to protect your friends from prosecution by the Colonial Survey. You're on your own, risking your life every minute of every day. You took a risk in not shooting me. Now you're risking more in going to help men who'd have to be witnesses that you were a criminal. What are you doing it for?"

Huyghens grinned.

"Because I don't like robots. I don't like the fact that they're subduing men, making men subordinate to them."

"Go on," insisted Bordman. "I don't see why disliking robots should make you a criminal! Nor men subordinating themselves to robots, either."

"But they are," said Huyghens mildly. "I'm a crank, of course. But — I live like a man on this planet. I go where I please and do what I please. My helpers are my friends. If the robot colony had been a success, would the humans in it have lived like men?

Hardly. They'd have lived the way robots let them! They'd have to stay inside a fence the robots built. They'd have to eat foods that robots could raise, and no others. Why, a man couldn't move his head near a window, because if he did the house-tending robots couldn't work! Robots would serve them — the way the robots determined — but all they'd get out of it would be jobs servicing robots!"

Bordman shook his head.

"As long as men want robot service, they have to take the service that robots can give. If you don't want those services —"

"I want to decide what I want," said Huyghens, again mildly, "instead of being limited to choose what I'm offered. In my home planet we halfway tamed it with dogs and guns. Then we developed the bears, and we finished the job with them. Now there's population-pressure and the room for bears and dogs — and men! — is dwindling. More and more people are being deprived of the power of decision, and being allowed only the power of choice among the things robots allow. The more we depend on robots, the more limited those choices become. We don't want our children to limit themselves to wanting what robots can provide! We don't want them shriveling to where they abandon everything robots can't give, or won't. We want them to be men and women. Not damned automatons who live *by* pushing robot-controls so they can live *to* push robot-controls. If that's not subordination to robots —"

"It's an emotional argument," protested Bordman. "Not everybody feels that way."

"But I feel that way," said Huyghens. "And so do a lot of others. This is a damned big galaxy and it's apt to contain some surprises. The one sure thing about a robot and a man who depends on them is that they can't handle the unexpected. There's going to come a time when we need men who can. So on my home planet, some of us asked for Loren Two, to colonize. It was refused — too dangerous. But men can colonize anywhere if they're men. So I came here to study the planet. Especially the sphexes. Eventually, we expected to ask for a license again, with proof that we could handle even those beasts. I'm already doing it in a mild way. But the Survey licensed a robot colony — and where is it?"

Bordman made a sour face.

"You took the wrong way to go about it, Huyghens. It was illegal. It is. It was the pioneer spirit, which is admirable enough, but wrongly directed. After all, it was pioneers who left Earth for the stars. But —"

Sourdough raised up on his hind-legs and sniffed the air. Huyghens swung his rifle around to be handy. Bordman slipped off the safety-catch on his own. Nothing happened.

"In a way," said Bordman, "you're talking about liberty and freedom, which most people think is politics. You say it can be more. In principle, I'll concede it. But the way you put it, it sounds like a freak religion."

"It's self-respect," corrected Huyghens.

"You may be —"

Faro Nell growled. She bumped Nugget with her nose, to drive him closer to Bordman. She snorted at him, and trotted swiftly to where Sitka and Sourdough faced toward the broader, sphex-filled expanse of the Sere Plateau. She took his position between them.

Huyghens gazed sharply beyond them and then all about.

"This could be bad!" he said softly. "But luckily there's no wind. Here's a sort of hill. Come along, Bordman!"

He ran ahead, Bordman following and Nugget plumping heavily with him. They reached the raised place, actually a mere hillock no more than five or six feet above the surrounding sand, with a distorted cactus-like growth protruding from the ground. Huyghens stared again. He used his binoculars.

"One sphex," he said curtly. "Just one! And it's out of all reason for a sphex to be alone. But it's not rational of them to gather in hundreds of thousands, either!" He whetted his finger and held it up. "No wind at all."

He used the binoculars again.

"It doesn't know we're here," he added. "It's moving away. Not another in sight. . . ." He hesitated, biting his lips. "Look here, Bordman. I'd like to kill that one lone sphex and find out something. There's a fifty percent chance I could find out something really important. But — I might have to run. If I'm right. . . ." Then he said grimly. "It'll have to be done quickly. I'm going to ride Faro Nell, for speed. I doubt Sitka or Sourdough will stay behind. But Nugget can't run fast enough. Will you stay here with him?"

Bordman drew in his breath. Then he said calmly:

"You know what you're doing, I hope."

"Keep your eyes open. If you see anything, even at a distance, shoot and we'll be back, fast! Don't wait until something's close enough to hit. Shoot the instant you see anything, if you do!"

Bordman nodded. He found it peculiarly difficult to speak again. Huyghens went over to the embattled bears and climbed up on Faro Nell's back, holding fast by her shaggy fur.

"Let's go!" he snapped. "That way! Hup!"

The three Kodiaks plunged away at a dead run, Huyghens lurching and swaying on Faro Nell's back. The sudden rush dislodged Semper from his perch. He flapped wildly and got aloft. Then he followed effortlessly, flying low.

It happened very quickly. A Kodiak bear can travel as fast as a racehorse on occasion. These three plunged arrow-straight for a spot perhaps half a mile distant, where a blue-and-tawny shape whirled to face them. There was the crash of Huyghens' weapon from where he rode on Faro Nell's back; the explosion of the weapon and the bullet was one sound. The monster leaped and died.

Huyghens jumped down from Faro Nell. He became feverishly busy at something on the ground. Semper banked and whirled and landed. He watched, with his head on one side.

Bordman stared. Huyghens was doing something to the dead sphex. The two male bears prowled about, while Faro Nell regarded Huyghens with intense curiosity. Back at the hillock, Nugget whimpered a little, and Bordman patted him. Nugget whimpered more loudly. In the distance, Huyghens straightened up and mounted Faro Nell's back. Sitka looked back toward Bordman. He reared upward. He made a noise, apparently, because Sourdough ambled to his side. The two great beasts began to trot back. Semper flapped wildly and — lacking wind — lurched crazily in the air. He landed on Huyghens' shoulder and clung there with his talons.

Then Nugget howled hysterically and tried to swarm up Bordman, as a cub tries to swarm up the nearest tree in time of danger. Bordman collapsed, and the cub upon him — and there was a flash of stinking scaly hide, while the air was filled with the snarling, spitting squeals of a sphex in full leap. The beast had over-jumped, aiming at Bordman and the cub while both were upright and arriving when they had fallen. It went tumbling.

Bordman heard nothing but the fiendish squalling, but in the distance Sitka and Sourdough were coming at rocket-ship speed. Faro Nell let out a roar that fairly split the air. And then there was a furry streaking toward her, bawling, while Bordman rolled to his feet and snatched up his gun. He raged through pure instinct. The sphex crouched to pursue the cub and Bordman swung his weapon as a club. He was literally too close to shoot — and perhaps the sphex had only seen the fleeing bear-cub. But he swung furiously —

And the sphex whirled. Bordman was toppled from his feet. An eight-hundred-pound monstrosity straight out of hell — half wildcat and half spitting cobra with hydrophobia and homicidal mania added — such a monstrosity is not to be withstood when in whirling its body strikes one in the chest.

That was when Sitka arrived, bellowing. He stood on his hind legs, emitting roars like thunder, challenging the sphex to battle. He waddled forward. Huyghens approached, but he could not shoot with Bordman in the sphere of an explosive bullet's destructiveness. Faro Nell raged and snarled, torn between the urge to be sure that Nugget was unharmed, and the frenzied fury of a mother whose offspring has been endangered.

Mounted on Faro Nell, with Semper clinging idiotically to his shoulders, Huyghens watched helplessly as the sphex spat and squalled at Sitka, having only to reach out one claw to let out Bordman's life.

They got away from there, though Sitka seemed to want to lift the limp carcass of his victim in his teeth and dash it repeatedly to the ground. He seemed doubly raging because a man — with whom all Kodius Champion's descendants had an emotional relationship — had been mishandled. But Bordman was not grievously hurt. He bounced and swore as the bears raced for the horizon. Huyghens had flung him up on Sourdough's pack and snapped for him to hold on. He shouted:

"Damn it, Huyghens! This isn't right! Sitka got some deep scratches! That horror's claws may be poisonous!"

But Huyghens snapped "Hup! Hup!" to the bears, and they continued to race against time. They went on for a good two miles, when Nugget wailed despairingly of his exhaustion and Faro Nell halted firmly to nuzzle him.

"This may be good enough," said Huyghens. "Considering that there's no wind and the big mass of beasts is down the plateau and there were only those two around here. Maybe they're too busy to hold a wake, even. Anyhow —"

He slid to the ground and extracted the antiseptic and swabs. "Sitka first," snapped Bordman. "I'm all right!"

Huyghens swabbed the big bear's wounds. They were trivial, because Sitka Pete was an experienced sphex-fighter. Then Bordman grudgingly let the curiously-smelling stuff — it reeked of ozone — be applied to the slashes on his chest. He held his breath as it stung. Then he said:

"It was my fault, Huyghens. I watched you instead of the landscape. I couldn't imagine what you were doing."

"I was doing a quick dissection," Huyghens told him. "By luck, the first sphex was a female, as I hoped. And she was about to lay her eggs. Ugh! And now I know why the sphexes migrate, and where, and how it is that they don't need game up here."

He slapped a quick bandage on Bordman, then led the way eastward, still putting distance between the dead sphexes and his party.

"I'd dissected them before," said Huyghens. "Not enough's been known about them. Some things needed to be found out if men were ever to be able to live here."

"With bears?" asked Bordman ironically.

"Oh, yes," said Huyghens. "Bu the point is that sphexes come to the desert here to breed, to mate and lay their eggs for the sun to hatch. It's a particular place. Seals return to a special place to mate — and the males, at least, don't eat for weeks on end. Salmon return to their native streams to spawn. They don't eat, and they die afterwards. And eels — I'm using Earth examples, Bordman — travel some thousands of miles to the Sargasso to mate and die. Unfortunately, sphexes don't appear to die, but it's clear that they have an ancestral breeding-place and that they come to the Sere Plateau to deposit their eggs!"

Bordman plodded onward. He was angry; angry with himself because he hadn't taken elementary precautions; because he'd felt too safe, as a man in a robot-served civilization forms the habit of doing; because he hadn't used his brains when Nugget whimpered, with even a bear-cub's awareness that danger was near.

"And now," Huyghens added, "I need some equipment that the robot colony has. With it, I think we can make a start toward turning this into a planet that men can live like men on!"

Bordman blinked.

"What's that?"

"Equipment," said Huyghens impatiently. "It'll be at the robot colony. Robots are useless because they wouldn't pay attention to sphexes. They'd still be. But take out the robot controls and the machines will do! They shouldn't be ruined by a few months exposure to weather!"

Bordman marched on and on. Presently he said:

"I never thought you'd want anything that came from that colony, Huyghens!"

"Why not?" demanded Huyghens impatiently. "When men make machines do what they want, that's all right. Even robots, when they're where they belong. But men will have to handle flame-casters in the job I want them for. There have to be some, because there was a hundred-mile clearing to be burned off for the colony. And earth-sterilizers, intended to kill the seeds of any plant that robots couldn't handle. We'll come back up here, Bordman, and at the least we'll destroy the spawn of these infernal beasts! If we can't do more than that, just doing that every year will wipe out the race in time. There are probably other hordes than this, with other breeding-places. But we'll find them too. We'll make this planet into a place where men from my world can come and still be men!"

Bordman said sardonically:

"It was sphexes that beat the robots. Are you sure you aren't planning to make this world safe for robots?"

Huyghens laughed.

"You've only seen one night-walker," he said. "And how about those things on the mountain-slope, which would have drained you of blood? Would you care to wander about this planet with only a robot bodyguard, Bordman? Men can't live on this planet with only robots to help them. You'll see!"

They found the colony after only ten days' more travel and after many sphexes and more than a few stag-like creatures and shaggy ruminants had fallen to their weapons and the bears. And they found survivors.

There were three of them, hard-bitten and bearded and deeply embittered. When the electrified fence went down, two of them were away at a mine tunnel, installing a new control panel for the robots who worked in it. The third was in charge of the mining operation. They were alarmed by the stopping of communication with the colony and went back in a tank-truck to find out what had happened, and only the fact that they were unarmed saved them. They found sphexes prowling and caterwauling about the fallen colony, in numbers they still did not wholly believe. The sphexes smelled men inside the armored vehicle, but couldn't break in. In turn, the men couldn't kill them, or they'd have been trailed to the mine and besieged there for as long as they could kill an occasional monster.

The survivors stopped all mining, of course, and tried to use remote-control robots for revenge and to get supplies for them. Their mining-robots were not designed for either task. And they had no weapons. They improvised miniature throwers of burning rocket-fuel, and they sent occasional prowling sphexes away screaming with scorched hides. But this was useful only because it did not kill the beasts. And it cost fuel. In the end they barricaded themselves and used the fuel only to keep a spark-signal going against the day when another ship came to seek the colony. They stayed in the mine as in a prison, on short rations, without real hope. For diversion they could only contemplate the mining-robots they could not spare fuel to run and which could not do anything but mine.

When Huyghens and Bordman reached them, they wept. They hated robots and all things robotic only a little less than they hated sphexes. But Huyghens explained, and, armed with weapons from the packs of the bears, they marched to the dead colony with the male Kodiaks as point and advance-guard, and with Faro Nell bringing up the rear. They killed sixteen sphexes on the way. In the now overgrown clearing there were four more. In the shelters of the colony they found only foulness and the fragments of what had been men. But there was some food — not much, because the sphexes clawed at anything that smelled of men, and had ruined the plastic packets of radiation-sterilized food. But there were some supplies in metal containers which were not destroyed.

And there was fuel, which men could use when they got to the control-panels for the equipment. There were robots everywhere, bright and shining and ready for operation, but immobile, with plants growing up around and over them.

They ignored those robots, and instead fueled tracked flame-casters — after adapting them to human rather than robot operation — and the giant soil-sterilizers which had been built to destroy vegetation that robots could not be made to weed out or cultivate. Then they headed back for the Sere Plateau.

As time passed Nugget became a badly spoiled bear-cub, because the freed men approved passionately of anything that would evern grow up to kill sphexes. They petted him to excess when they camped.

Finally they reached the plateau by the sphex-trail to the top and sphexes came squalling and spitting to destroy them. While Bordman and Huyghens fired steadily, the great machines swept up with their special weapons. The earth-sterilizer, it developed, was deadly against animal life as well as seeds, when its diathermic beam was raised and aimed.

Presently the bears were not needed, because the scorched corpses of sphexes drew live ones from all parts of the plateau even in the absence of noticeable breezes. The official business of the sphexes was presumably finished, but they came to caterwaul and seek vengeance — which they did not find. After a while the survivors of the robot colony drove the machines in great circles around the huge heap of slaughtered fiends, destroying new arrivals as they came. It was such a killing as men had never before made on any planet, and there would be very few left of the sphex-horde which had bred in this particular patch of desert.

Nor would more grow up, because the soil-sterilizer would go over the dug-up sand where the sphex-spawn lay hidden for the sun to hatch. And the sun would never hatch them.

Huyghens and Bordman, by that time, were camped on the edge of the plateau with the Kodiaks. Somehow it seemed more befitting for the men of the robot colony to conduct the slaughter. After all, it was those men whose companions had been killed.

There came an evening when Huyghens cuffed Nugget away from where he sniffed too urgently at a stag-steak cooking on the campfire. Nugget ambled dolefully behind the protecting form of Bordman and sniveled.

"Huyghens," said Bordman, "we've got to come to a settlement of our affairs. You're an illegal colonist, and it's my duty to arrest you."

Huyghens regarded him with interest.

"Will you offer me lenience if I tell on my confederates?" he asked. "Or may I plead that I can't be forced to testify against myself?"

Bordman said:

"It's irritating! I've been an honest man all my life, but — I don't believe in robots as I did, except in their place. And their place isn't here! Not as the robot colony was planned, anyhow. The sphexes are nearly wiped out, but they won't be extinct and robots can't handle them. Bears and men will have to live here or else the people who do will have to spend their lives behind sphex-proof fences, accepting only what robots can give them. And there's much too much on this planet for people to miss it! To live in a robot-managed environment on a planet like Loren Two wouldn't — it wouldn't be self-respecting!"

"You wouldn't be getting religious, would you?" asked Huyghens dryly. "That was your term for self-respect before."

"You don't let me finish!" protested Bordman. "It's my job to pass on the work that's done on a planet before any but the first-landed colonist may come there to live. And of course to see that specifications are followed. Now, the robot colony I was sent to survey was practically destroyed. As designed, it wouldn't work. It couldn't survive."

Huyghens grunted. Night was falling. He turned the meat over the fire.

"In emergencies," said Bordman, "colonists have the right to call on any passing ship for aid. Naturally! So my report will be that the colony as designed was impractical, and that it was over-whelmed and destroyed except for three survivors who holed up and signaled for help. They did, you know!"

"Go on," grunted Huyghens.

"So," said Bordman, "it just happened — just happened, mind you — that a ship with you and the bears and the eagle on board picked up the distress-call. So you landed to help the colonists. That's the story. Therefore it isn't illegal for you to be here. It was only illegal for you to be here when you were needed. But we'll pretend you weren't."

Huyghens glanced over his shoulder in the deepening night. He said:

"I wouldn't believe that if I told it myself. Do you think the Survey will?"

"They're not fools," said Bordman tartly. "Of course they won't! But when my report says that because of this unlikely series of events it is practical to colonize the planet, whereas before it wasn't, and when my report proves that a robot colony alone is stark nonsense, but that with bears and men from your world added, so many thousand colonists can be received per year. . . . And when that much is true, anyhow. . . ."

Huyghens seemed to shake a little as a dark silhouette against the flames.

"My reports carry weight," insisted Bordman. "The deal will be offered, anyhow! The robot colony organizers will have to agree or they'll have to fold up. And your people can hold them up for nearly what terms they choose."

Huyghens' shaking became understandable. It was laughter.

"You're a lousy liar, Bordman," he said. "Isn't it unintelligent and unreasonable to throw away a lifetime of honesty just to get me out of a jam? You're not acting like a rational animal, Bord-man. But I thought you wouldn't when it came to the point."

Bordman squirmed.

"That's the only solution I can think of," he said. "But it'll work."

"I accept it," said Huyghens, grinning. "With thanks. If only because it means another few generations of men can live like men on a planet that is going to take a lot of taming. And — if you want to know — because it keeps Sourdough and Sitka and Nell and Nugget from being killed because I brought them here illegally."

Something pressed hard against Bordman. Nugget, the cub, pushed urgently against him in his desire to get closer to the fragrantly cooking meat. He edged forward. Bordman toppled from where he squatted on the ground. He sprawled. Nugget sniffed luxuriously.

"Slap him," said Huyghens. "He'll move back."

"I won't!" said Bordman indignantly from where he lay. "I won't do it. He's my friend!"

It was ironic that, after all, Bordman found that he couldn't afford to retire. His pay, of course, had been used to educate his children and maintain his home. And Lani III was an expensive world to live on. It was now occupied by a thriving, bustling populations with keen business instincts, and the vapor-curtains about it were commonplace, now, and few people remembered a time when they hadn't existed — when it was a world below habitability for anybody. So Bordman wasn't a hero. As a matter of history he was simply a citizen who could be interviewed for visicasts on holidays, but hadn't much that was new to say.

But he lived on Lani III for three years, and he was restless. His children were grown and married, now, — and they hadn't known him too well, anyhow. He'd been away so much! He didn't fit into the world whose green fields and oceans and rivers he was responsible for. But it was infinitely good to be with Riki again. There was so much that each remembered, to be shared with the other, that they had plenty to talk about.

Three years after his official retirement, he was asked to take on another Survey job on which there was no other qualified man free to work on. He talked to his wife. On retirement pay, life was not easy, now. Her children were safely on their own. Bordman would always need her. She advised him for both their sakes. And he went back to Survey duty with the stipulation that he should have quarters and facilities for his wife as well as himself on all assignments.

They had five wonderful years. Bordman was near the top of the ladder, then. His children wrote faithfully. He was busy on Kelmin IV, and his wife had a garden there, when he was summoned to Sector Headquarters with first priority urgency.

# IV

## THE SWAMP WAS UPSIDE DOWN

Bordman knew the Survey ship had turned end for end, because though there was artificial gravity, it does not affect the semicircular canals of the human ear. He knew he was turning head-over-heels, even though his feet stayed firmly on the floor. It was not a normal sensation, and he felt a little queasy, instinctive tightening of the muscles with which one reacts to the abnormal, whether in things seen or felt.

But the reason for turning the ship end-for-end was obvious. It had arrived very near its destination, and was killing the Lawlor drive momentum. Just as Bordman was assured that the turning motion was finished, young Barnes — the ship's lowest-ranking commissioned officer — came into the wardroom and beamed at him.

"The ship's not landing, sir," he said, like one explaining something to somebody under ten years old. "Our orders are changed. You're to go to ground by boat. This way, sir."

Bordman shrugged. He was a Senior Officer of the Colonial Survey, grown old in the Service, and this was a Survey ship that had been sent especially to get him from his last and still unfinished job. It was a top-urgency matter. The ship had had no other business for some months except to go after him and bring him to Sector Headquarters, down on Canna III, which must be somewhere near. But this young officer was patronizing him!

Bordman rather ruefully recognized that he didn't know how to be impressive. He was not a good salesman of his own importance. He didn't even get the respect due his rank.

Now the young officer waited, brisk and alert. Bordman reflected wryly that he could pin young Barnes' ears back easily enough. But he remembered when he'd been a junior Survey ship's officer. Then he'd felt a bland condescension toward all people of whatever rank who did not spend their lives in the cramped, skimped quarters of a Survey patrol-ship. If this young Lieutenant Barnes was fortunate, he'd always feel that way. Bordman could not begrudge him the cockiness which made the tedium and hardships of the Service seem to him a privilege.

So he obediently followed Barnes through the wardroom door. He ducked his head under a ventilation-slot and sidled past a standpipe with bristling air-valve handles. It almost closed the way. There was the smell of oil and paint and ozone which all proper Survey ships maintain in their working sections.

"Here, sir," said Barnes. "This way."

He offered his arm for Bordman to steady himself. Bordman ignored it. He stepped over a complex of white-painted pipes, and arrived at an almost clear way to a boat-blister.

"And your luggage, sir," added the young man reassuringly, "will follow you down immediately, sir. With the mail."

Bordman nodded. He moved toward the blister door. He sidled past constrictions due to new equipment. The Survey ship had been designed a long time ago, and there were no funds for rebuilding when improved devices came along. So any Survey ship was apt to be cluttered up with afterthoughts in metal.

A speaker from the wall said sharply:

*"Hear this! Hold fast! Gravity going off!"*

Bordman caught a nearby pipe, and snatched his hand away again — it was hot — and caught on to another and then put his other hand below. He applied a trifle of pressure. The young officer said kindly:

"Hold fast, sir. If I may suggest —"

The gravity did go off. Bordman grimaced. There'd been a time when he was used to such matters, but this time the sudden outward surge of his breath caught him unprepared. His diaphragm contracted as the weight of organs above it ceased to be. He choked for an instant. He said evenly:

"I am not likely to go head-over-heels, Lieutenant. I served four years as a junior swot on a ship exactly like this!"

He did not float about. He held onto a pipe in two places, and he applied expert pressure in a strictly professional manner, and his feet remained firmly on the floor. He startled young Barnes by this achievement, which only junior swots think only junior swots know about.

Barnes said, abashed. "Yes, sir." He held himself in the same fashion.

"I even know," said Bordman, "that the gravity had to be cut off because we're approaching another ship on Lawlor drive. Our gravity-coils would blow if we got into her field with our drive off, or if her field pressed ours inboard."

Young Barnes looked extremely uncomfortable. Bordman felt sorry for him. To be chewed, however delicately, for patronizing a senior officer could not be pleasant. So Bordman added:

"And I also remember that, when I was a junior swot, I once tried to tell a Sector Chief how to top off his suit-tanks. So don't let it bother you!"

The young officer was embarrassed. A Sector Chief was so high in the table of Survey organization that one of his idle thoughts was popularly supposed to be able to crack a junior officer's skull. If Bordman, as a young officer, had really tried to tell a Sector Chief how to top his suit-tanks. . . . Why. . . .

"Thank you, sir," said Barnes awkwardly. "I'll try not to be an ass again, sir."

"I suspect," said Bordman, "that you'll slip occasionally. I did! What the devil's another ship doing out here and why aren't we landing?"

"I wouldn't know, sir," said the young officer. His manner toward Bordman was quite changed. "I do know the Skipper came in expecting to land by landing-grid, sir. He was told to stand off. He's as much surprised as you are, sir."

The wall-speaker said crisply:

*"Hear this! Gravity returning! Gravity returning!"*

And weight came back. Bordman was ready for it this time and took it casually. He looked at the speaker and it said nothing more. He nodded to the young man.

"I suppose I'd better get in the boat. No change in that arrangement, anyhow!"

He crawled through the blister door and wormed his way into the landing boat, one designed for a more modern ship, and excessively inconvenient in such an outmoded launching-device. Barnes crawled in after him.

He dogged the blister door from the inside, closed the boat-port and dogged it, and flipped a switch.

"Excuse me, sir. I'm to take you down."

"Ready for departure," he said into a microphone.

A dial on the instrument-board flicked halfway to zero. It stopped there. Seconds passed. A green light glowed. The young officer said:

"All tight!"

The needle darted a quarter-way further over, and then began to descend slowly. The blister was being pumped empty of air. Presently another light glowed.

"Ready for launching," said the young officer briskly.

The blister-seal broke with a clank, and the two halves of the boat-cover drew back. There were stars. To Bordman they were unfamiliarly arranged, but he could have picked out Seton and the Donis cluster in any case, and half a hundred more markers by taking thought of the position of the planet Canna III, on which

Colonial Survey Sector Headquarters for this part of the galaxy were established.

The boat moved out of its place, and the ship's gravity-field ended as abruptly as such fields do.

The Survey ship floated away, as seen from the vision-ports of the boat. It apparently increased its drive, because the boat swirled and swayed as changing eddy-currents moved it. The ship grew small and vanished. The boat hung in emptiness, turning slowly. The sun Canna came into view. It was very large for a Sol-type sun, and its rim was almost devoid of the prominences and jet-streams of flaming gas that older suns of the type display. But even out at the third orbit it provided O-1 climate — optimum: equivalent to Earth — for the planet below.

That planet now came swinging into view as the ship's boat continued to turn. It was blue. More than ninety percent of its surface was water, and much of the solid land was under its northern ice-cap. It had been chosen as Sector Headquarters because of its unsuitability for a large population, which might resent the considerable land-area needed for Survey storage and reserve facilities.

Bordman regarded it thoughtfully. The boat was, of course, roughly five planetary diameters out, the conventional distance to which a ship approached any planet on its own drive. Bordman could see the ice-cap clearly, and blue sea beyond it, and the twi-light line. There was one cyclonic storm just dissipating toward the night-side, and the edge of a similar cloud-system down toward the equator. Bordman searched for Headquarters. It was on an island at about forty-five degrees latitude, which ought to be near the center of the planet's surface as seen from where the ship's boat floated. But he could not make it out. There was only the one island of any importance and it was not large.

Nothing happened. The boat's rockets remained silent. The young officer sat quietly, looking at the instruments before him. He seemed to be waiting for something to happen.

A needle kicked and stayed just off the pin. It was an external-field indicator. Some field, somewhere, now included the space in which the ship's boat floated.

"Hm," said Bordman. "You're waiting for orders?"

"Yes, sir," said the young man. "I'm ordered not to land except under ground instructions, sir. I don't know why."

Bordman observed:

"One of the worst wiggings I ever got was in a boat like this. I was waiting for orders and they didn't come. I acted very Service about it: stiff upper lip and all that. But I was getting in serious trouble when it occurred to me that it might be my fault I wasn't getting the orders."

The young officer glanced quickly at the instrument he had previously ignored. Then he said relievedly:

"Not this time, sir. The communicator's turned on all right."

Bordman said:

"Do you think they might be calling you without shifting from ship-frequency? They were talking to the ship, you know."

"I'll try, sir."

The young man leaned forward and switched to ship-band adjustment of the communicator. Different wave-bands, naturally, were used between the ship and shore, and a ship and its own boats. A booming carrier wave came on instantly. The young officer hastily turned down the volume and words became distinguishable.

"... *What the devil's the matter with you? Acknowledge!*"

The young officer gulped. Bordman said mildly:

"Since he ranks you, just say 'sorry, sir.'"

"S-sorry, sir," said Barnes into the microphone.

"*Sorry?*" snapped the voice from the ground. "*I've been calling for five minutes! Your skipper will hear about this! I shall —*"

Bordman pulled the microphone before him.

"My name is Bordman," he observed. "I am waiting for instructions to land. My pilot has been listening on boat-frequency, as was proper. You appear to be calling us on an improper channel. Really —"

There was stricken silence. Then babbled apologies from the speaker. Bordman smiled faintly at young Barnes.

"It's quite all right. Let's forget it now. But will you give my pilot his instructions?"

The voice said with strained formality:

"You're to be brought down by landing-grid, sir. Rocket-landings have been ruled non-permitted by the Sector Chief himself, sir. But we are already landing one boat, sir. Senior Officer Werner is being brought in now, sir. His boat is still two diameters out, sir, and it will take us nearly an hour to get him down without extreme discomfort, sir."

"Then we'll wait," said Bordman. "Hm. Call us again before you start hunting us with the landing-beam. My pilot has a rather promising idea. And will you call us on the proper frequency then, please?"

The voice aground said unhappily, "Yes, sir. Certainly, sir."

The carrier-wave hum stopped. Young Barnes said gratefully:

"Thank you, sir! Hell hath no fury like a ranking officer caught in a blunder! He'd have twisted my tail for his mistake, sir, and it could have been bad!" Then he paused. He said uneasily. "But — beg pardon, sir. I haven't any promising ideas. Not that I know of!"

"You have an hour to develop one," Bordman told him.

Internally, Bordman was startled. There were few occasions on which even one Senior Officer was called in to Sector Headquarters. Interstellar distances being what they were, and thirty light-speeds being practically the best available, Senior Officers necessarily acted pretty much as independent authorities. To call one man in meant all his other work had to go by the board for a matter of months. But two! And Werner?

Werner was getting to ground first. If there was something serious ashore, Werner would make a great point of arriving first, even if only by hours. A keen sort of person in giving the right impression. He'd risen in the Service faster than Bordman. The other Lawlor field would have been his ship getting out of the way.

The young officer at his elbow fidgeted.

"Beg pardon, sir. What sort of idea should I develop, sir? I'm not sure I understand —"

"It's rather annoying to have to stay parked in free fall," said Bordman patiently. "And it's always a good practice to review annoying situations and see if they can be bettered."

Barnes' forehead wrinkled.

"We could land much quicker on rockets, sir. And even when the landing-grid reaches out for us, they'll have to handle us very cautiously or they'd break our necks, since we've no gravity coils."

Bordman nodded. Barnes was thinking straight enough, but it takes young officers a long time to think of thinking straight. They have to obey so many orders unquestioningly that they tend to stop doing anything else. Yet at each rise in grade some slight trace of increased capacity to think is required. In order to reach really high rank, an officer has to be capable of thinking which simply isn't possible unless he's kept in practice on the way up.

Young Barnes looked up, startled.

"Look here, sir!" he said, surprised. "If it takes them an hour to let down Senior Officer Werner from two planetary diameters, it'll take much longer to let us down from out here!"

"True," said Bordman.

"And you don't want to spend three hours descending, sir, after waiting an hour for him!"

"I don't," admitted Bordman. He could have given orders, of course. But if a junior officer was spurred to the practice of thinking, it meant that some day he'd be a better senior officer. And Bordman knew how desperately few men were really adequate for high authority. Anything that could be done to increase the number —

Bordman nodded again.

"So by the time they've got that other boat landed — why — I can use rockets and get down to one diameter myself, sir! And they can lock onto us there and let us down a few thousand miles only. So we can get to ground half an hour after the other boat's down instead of four hours from now."

"Just so," agreed Bordman. "At a cost of little thought and a little fuel. You have a promising idea after all, Lieutenant. Suppose you carry it out?"

Young Barnes glanced at Bordman's safety-strap. He threw over the fuel-ready lever and conscientiously waited the few seconds for the first molecules of fuel to be catalyzed cold. Once firing started, they'd be warmed to detonation-readiness in the last few millimeters of the injection-gap.

"Firing, sir," he said respectfully.

There was the curious sound of a rocket blasting in emptiness, when the sound is conveyed only by the rocket-tube's metal. There was the smooth, pushing sensation of acceleration. They tiny ship's boat swung and aimed down at the planet. Lieutenant Barnes leaned forward and punched the ship's computer.

"I hope you'll excuse me, sir," he said. "I should have thought that out myself without prompting. But problems like this don't turn up very often, sir. As a rule it's wisest to follow precedents as if they were orders."

Bordman said dryly:

"To be sure! But one reason for the existence of junior officers is the fact that some day there will have to be new senior ones."

Barnes considered. Then he said surprisedly:

"I never thought of it that way, sir. Thank you."

He continued to punch the computer keys, frowning. Bordman relaxed in his seat, held there by the gentle acceleration and the belt. He'd had nothing by which to judge the reason for his summoning to Headquarters. He had very little now. But there was trouble of some sort down below. Two senior officers dragged from their own work. Werner now. . . . Bordman preferred not to estimate Werner. He disliked the man, and would be biased. But he was able, though definitely on the make. And there was himself. They'd been called to a headquarters where no ship was to be landed by landing-grid, nor any rocket to come to ground. A landing-grid could pluck a ship out of space ten planet-diameters out, and draw it with gentle violence shoreward, and land it lightly as a feather. A landing-grid could take the heaviest, loaded freighter and stop it in orbit and bring it down at eight gravities. But the one below wouldn't land even a tiny Survey ship! And a landing-boat was forbidden to come down on its rockets!

Bordman arranged those items in his mind. He knew the planet below, of course. When he got his Senior rating, he'd spent six months at Headquarters learning procedures and practices proper to his increased authority. There was one inhabitable island, two hundred miles long and possibly forty wide. There was no other useable ground outside the Arctic. The one occupied island had gigantic sheer cliffs on its windward side, where a great slab of bedrock had split along some submarine fault and tilted upward above the surface. Those cliffs were four thousand feet high, and from them the island sloped very gently and very gradually until its leeward shore slipped under the restless sea. Sector Headquarters had been placed here because it seemed that civilians would not want to colonize so limited a world. But there were citizens, because there was Headquarters. And now every inch of ground was cultivated, and there was irrigation and intensive farming and some hydroponic establishments. However, Sector Headquarters included a vast reserve area on which a space-fleet might be marshaled in case of need. The overcrowded civilians were bitter because of the great uncultivated area the Survey needed for storage and possible emergency use. Even when Bordman was here, years back, there was bitterness because the Survey crowded the civil economy which had been based on it.

Bordman considered all these items, and came to an uncomfortable conclusion. Presently he looked up. The planet loomed larger. Much larger.

"I think you'd better lose all planet-ward velocity before we hook on," he observed. "The landing-grid crew might have trouble focussing on us so close if we're moving."

"Yes, sir," said the young officer.

"There's some sort of merry hell below," said Bordman. "It looks bad that they won't let a ship come down by grid. It looks worse that they won't let this one land on its rockets." He paused. "I doubt they'll risk lifting us off again."

Young Barnes finished his computations. He looked satisfied. He glanced at the now-gigantic planet below, and deftly adjusted the course of the tiny boat. Then he jerked his head around.

"Excuse me, sir. Did you say we mightn't be able to lift off again?"

"I could almost predict that we won't," said Bordman.

"Would you — could you say why, sir?"

"They don't want landings. The trouble is here. If they don't want landings, they won't want launchings. Werner and I were sent for, so presumably we're needed. But apparently there's un-easiness about even our landing. They won't send us off again. I suspect —"

The loud-speaker said tinnily:

*"Calling boat for landing-grid! Calling boat for landing-grid!"*

"Come in," said Barnes, looking uneasily at Bordman.

*"Correct your course!"* commanded the voice. *"You are not to land on rockets under any circumstances! This is an order from the Senior Chief himself. Stand off! We will be ready to lock on and land you gently in about fifteen minutes. But meanwhile, stand off!"*

"Yes, sir," said Barnes, looking uneasily at Bordman.

Bordman reached over and took the microphone.

"Bordman speaking," he said. "I'd like information. What's the trouble down there that we can't use our rockets?"

"Rockets are noisy, sir. Even boat-rockets. We have orders to eliminate all physical vibration possible, sir. But I am ordered not to give details on a transmitter, sir."

"I sign off," said Bordman, dryly.

He pushed the microphone away. He deplored his own lack of aggressiveness. Werner, now, would have pulled his rank and insisted on being informed. But Bordman couldn't help believing that there was a reason for orders that overruled his own.

The young officer swung the rocket end-for-end. The sensa-tion of pressure against the back of Bordman's seat increased.

Minutes later, the speaker said.

"Grid to boat. Prepare for lock-on."

"Ready, sir," said Barnes.

The small boat shuddered and leaped crazily. It spun. It oscillated violently through seconds-long arcs in emptiness. Very gradually the oscillations died. There was a momentary sen-sation of the faint tugging of planetary weight, which is somehow subtly different from the feel of artificial gravity. Then the cosmos turned upside down as the boat was drawn swiftly toward the watery planet below it.

Some minutes later, young Barnes spoke:

"Beg pardon, sir," he said apologetically. "I must be stupid, sir, but I can't imagine any reason why vibrations or noises should make any difference on a planet. How could it do harm?"

"This is an ocean-planet," said Bordman. "It might make people drown."

The young officer flushed and turned his head away. And Bordman reflected that the young were always sensitive. But he did not speak again. When they landed in the spidery, half-mile-high landing-grid, Barnes would find out whether he was right or not.

He did. And Bordman was right. The people on Canna III were anxious to avoid vibrations because they were afraid of drowning.

Their fears seemed to be rather well-founded.

Three hours after landing, Bordman moved gingerly over grayish muddy rock, with a four-thousand-foot sheer drop some twenty yards away. The ragged edge of a cliff fell straight down for the better part of a mile. Far below, the sea rippled gently. Bordman saw a long, long line of boats moving slowly out to sea. They towed something between them which reached from boat to boat in exaggerated catenary curves. The boats moved in line abreast straight out from the cliffs, towing this floating, curved thing between them.

Bordman regarded them for a moment and then inspected the graying mud underfoot. He lifted his eyes to the inland side of this peculiar stretch of mountainside muddiness. There was a mast on the rock not far away. It held up what looked like a vision camera.

Young Barnes said:

"Excuse me, sir. What are those boats doing?"

"They're towing an oil-slick to sea," said Bordman absently, "by towing a floating line of some sort between them. There isn't enough oil to maintain the slick, and it's blown landward. So they tow it out to sea again. It holds down the seas. Every time, of course, they lose some of it."

"But —"

"There are trade-winds," said Bordman, not looking to sea-ward at all. "They always blow in the same direction, nearly. They blow three-quarters of the way around the planet, and they build up seas as they blow. Normally, the swells that pound against the cliff, here, will be a hundred feet and more from trough to crest. They'll throw spray ten times that high, of course, and once when I was here before, spray came over the cliff-tops. The impacts of the waves are — heavy. In a storm, if you put your ear to the ground on the leeward shore, you can hear the waves smash against these cliffs. It's vibration."

Barnes looked uneasily at the cliff's edge and the line of boats pushing over an ocean whose waves seemed less than ripples from nearly a mile above them. But the line of boats was incredibly long. It was twenty miles in length at the least.

"The slick holds down the waves," Barnes guessed. "It works best in deep water, I believe. The ancients knew it. Oil on the waters." He considered. "Working hard to prevent vibrations! Are they really so dangerous, sir?"

Bordman nodded inland. A quarter mile from the edge of the cliff there was a peculiar, broken, riven rampart of soil. It might have been forty feet high, once. Now it was shattered and cracked. It had the look of having been pulled away from where it was withdrawn. There were vertical breaks in its edges and broken-off masses left behind. At one place, a clump of perhaps a quarter-acre had not followed the rest, and trees leaned drunkenly from its top, and at the edge had fallen outward. All along the top of the stone cliff as far as the eye could see there was this singular retreat of soil and vegetation from the cliff's edge.

Bordman stopped and picked up a bit of the mud underfoot. He rubbed it between his fingers. It yielded like modeling clay. He dipped a finger into a gray, greasy-seeming puddle. He looked at the thick liquid on his finger and then rubbed it against his other palm. Young Barnes duplicated this last action.

"It feels soapy, sir!" he said blankly. "Like wet soap!"

"Yes," said Bordman. "That's the first problem here."

He turned to a ground-service Survey private, and jerked his head along the coastline.

"How much have other places slipped?"

"Anywhere from this much, sir," said the private, "to two miles and upward. There's one place where it's moving at a regular rate. Four inches an hour, sir. It was three-and-a-half yesterday."

Bordman nodded.

"Hm. We'll go back to Headquarters. Nasty business!"

He plodded over the messy footing toward the vehicle which had brought him here. It was not an ordinary ground-car. Instead of wires or caterwheels, it rolled upon flaccid, partly-inflated five-foot rollers. They would be completely unaffected by roughness or slipperiness of terrain and if the vehicle fell overboard it would float. It was thickly coated with the gray mud from the cliff-top.

As he moved along, Bordman was able to see the pattern of the rock underneath the mud. It was curiously contorted, like something that had curdled rather than cooled. And, as a matter of fact, it was believed to have solidified slowly under water at such monstrous pressure that even molten rock could not make it burst into steam. But it was above-water now.

Bordman climbed into the vehicle, and Barnes followed him. The bolster-truck turned and moved toward the broken barrier of earth. Its five-foot flabby rollers seemed rather to flow over than surmount obstacles. Great lumps of drier dirt dented them and did not disintegrate. There were no stones.

Bordman frowned to himself. The bolster-truck more or less flowed up the crumbling, inexplicably drawing-back mass of soil. Atop it, things looked almost normal. Almost. There was a highway leading away from the cliff. At first glance it seemed perfect. But it was cracked down the middle for a hundred yards, and then the crack meandered off to the side and was gone. There was a great tree, which leaned drunkenly. A mile along the roadway its surface buckled as if something had pressed irresistibly upward from below. The truck rolled over the break.

It was notable that the motion of the truck was utterly smooth. It made no vibration at all. But even so it slowed before it moved through a place where buildings — houses and a shop or two — clustered closely together on each side of the road.

There were people in and about the house, but they were doing nothing at all. Some of them stared at the Survey truck with hostility. Some others deliberately turned their backs to it. There were vehicles out of shelter and ready to be used, but none was moving. All were pointed in the direction from which the bolster-truck had come.

The truck went on. Presently the extraordinary flatness of the landscape became apparent. It was possible to see a seemingly illimitable distance. The ocean forty miles away showed as a thread of blue beneath the horizon. The island was an almost perfectly plane tilted surface. There was no hill visible anywhere, nor any valleys save the extremely minor gullies worn by rain. Even they had been filled in, dammed, and tied in to irrigation systems.

There was a place where there was a row of trees along such a water-course. Half the row had fallen, and a part of the rest was tilted. The remainder stood upright and firm. All the vegetation was perfectly familiar. Most colonies have some vegetation, at least, directly descended from the mother planet Earth. But this island on Canna III had been above-water perhaps no more than three or four thousand years. There had been no time for local vegetation to develop. When the Survey took it over, there was nothing but tidal seaweed, only one variety of which had been able to extend itself in a web-like fashion over the soil above water. Terrestrial plants had wiped it out, and everything was green and human-introduced.

But there was something wrong with the ground. At this place the top of the soil bulged, and tall corn-plants grew extravagantly in different directions. At another, there was a narrow, lipless gash in the ground's surface. An irrigation-ditch poured water into it. It was not filled.

Barnes said:

"Excuse me, sir, but how the devil did this happen?"

"There's been irrigation," said Bordman patiently. "The soil here was all ocean-bottom, once — it used to be what is called globigerinous ooze. There's no sand, and no stones. There's only bedrock and formerly abyssal mud. And some of it underneath is no longer former. It's globigerinous ooze again."

He waved his hand at the landscape. It had been remarkably tidy, once. Every square foot of ground had been cultivated. The highways were limited width, and the houses were neat and trim. It was, perhaps, the most completely civilized landscape in the galaxy. Bordman added:

"You said the stuff felt like soap. In a way it's acting like soap. It lies on slightly slanting, effectively smooth rock, like a soap-cake on a sheet of metal that's tilted a bit. And that's the trouble. So long as a cake of soap is dry on the bottom it doesn't move. Even if you pour water on top, like rain, the top will wet, and the water will flow off, but the bottom won't wet until all the soap is dissolved away. While that was the process here, everything was all right. But they've been irrigating."

They passed a row of neat cottages facing the road. One had collapsed completely. The other looked absolutely normal. The bolster-truck went on.

Bordman said, frowning:

"They wanted the water to go into the soil, so they arranged it. A little of that did no harm. Plants growing dried it out again. One tree evaporates thousands of gallons a day in a good trade-wind. There were some landslides in the early days, especially when storm-swells pounded the cliffs, but on the whole the ground was more firmly anchored when first cultivated than it had been before the colonists came."

"But irrigation? The sea's not fresh, is it?"

"Water-freshening plants," said Bordman dryly. "Ion-exchange systems. They installed them and had all the fresh water they could wish for. And they wished for a lot. They deepploughed, so the water would sink in. They dammed the watercourses. What they did amounted to something like boring holes in that cake of soap I used for an illustration just now. Water went right down to the bottom. What would happen then?"

Barnes said:

"Why, the bottom would get wet — and the soap would slide! As if it were greased!"

"Not greased," corrected Bordman. "Soaped. Soap is viscous. That's different, and a lucky difference, too. But the least vibration would encourage movement. And it does. So the population is now walking on eggs. Worse, it's walking on the equivalent of a cake of soap which is getting wetter and wetter on the bottom. It's already sliding as a viscous substance does, reluctantly. But in spite of the oil-slick they're trying to keep in place upwind there's still some battering from the sea. There are still some vibrations in the bedrock. And so there's a slow, gentle, gradual sliding."

"And they figure," said Barnes, "that locking onto a ship with the landing-grid might be like an earthquake." He stopped. "An earthquake, now —"

"Not much vulcanism on this planet," Bordman told him. "But of course there are tectonic quakes occasionally. They made this island."

Barnes said uneasily:

"I don't think, sir, that I'd sleep well if I lived here."

"You are living here for the moment. But at your age I think you'll sleep."

The bolster-truck turned, following he highway. The road was very even, and the motion of the truck along it was infinitely smooth. Its lack of vibration explained why it was permitted to move when all other vehicles were stopped. But Bordman reflected uneasily that this did not account for the orders of the Sector Chief forbidding the rocket-landing of a ship's boat. It was true enough that the living-surface of the island rested upon slanting stone, and that if the bottom were wet enough it could slide off into the sea. It already had moved. At least one place was moving at four inches per hour. But that was viscous flow. It would be enhanced by vibration, and assuredly the hammering of seas upon the windward cliff should be lessened by any possible means.

But it did not mean that the sound of a rocket-landing would be disastrous, nor the straining of a landing-grid as it stopped a spaceship in orbit and drew it to ground should produce a landslide. There was something else, though the situation for the island's civilian population was already serious enough. If any really massive movement of the ground did begin, viscous or any other, if any considerable part of the island's surface did begin to move, all of it would go. And the population would go with it. If there were survivors, they would be numbered in dozens.

The tall tamped-earth wall of the Headquarters reserve area loomed ahead. Sector Headquarters had been established here when there were no other inhabitants. Seeds had been broadcast and trees planted while the Survey buildings were under construction. Headquarters, in fact, had been built upon an uninhabited planet. But colonists followed in the wake of Survey personnel. Wives and children, and then storekeepers and agriculturists, and presently civilian technicians and ultimately even politicians arrived as the non-Service population grew. Now Sector Headquarters was resented because it occupied one-fourth of the island. It kept too much of the planet's useful surface out of civilian use. And the island was desperately overcrowded.

But it seemed also to be doomed.

As the bolster-truck moved silently toward Headquarters, a hundred-yard section of the wall collapsed. There was an upsurging of dust, and a rumbling of falling, hardened dirt. The truck's driver turned white. A civilian beside the road faced the wall and wrung his hands, and stood waiting to feel the ground under his feet begin to sweep smoothly toward the here-distant sea. A post held up a traffic signal some twenty yards from the gate. It leaned slowly. At a forty-five-degree tilt it checked and hung stationary. Fifty yards from the gate, a new crack appeared across the road.

But nothing more happened. Nothing. Yet one could not be sure that some critical point had not been passed, so that from now on there wold be a gradual rise in the creeping of the soil toward the ocean.

Barnes caught his breath.

"That makes me feel — queer," he said unsteadily. "A shock like that wall falling could start everything off!"

Bordman said nothing at all. It had occurred to him that there was no irrigation of the Survey area. He frowned thoughtfully, even worriedly, as the truck went inside the Headquarters gate and rolled on over a winding road through park-like surroundings.

It stopped before the building which was the Sector Chief's

own headquarters in Headquarters. A large brown dog dozed peacefully on the plastic-tiled landing at the top of half a dozen steps. When Bordman got out of the truck the dog got up with a leisurely air. And when Bordman ascended the steps, with Barnes following him, the dog came forward with a sort of stately courtesy to do the honors. Bordman said:

"Nice dog, that."

He went inside. The dog followed. The interior of the building was empty, and there was a sort of resonant silence until somewhere a telewriter began to click.

"Come along," said Bordman. "The Sector Chief's office is over this way."

Young Barnes followed.

"It seems odd there's no one around," he said. "No secretaries, no sentries, nobody at all."

"Why should there be?" asked Bordman in surprise. "The guards at the gate keep civilians out. And nobody in the Service will bother the Chief without reason. At least, no more than once!"

But across the glistening, empty floor there ran an ominous crack.

They went down a corridor. Voices sounded, and Bordman tracked them, with the paws of the dog clicking on the floor behind him. He led the way into a spacious, comfortable nondescript room with high windows — doors, really — that opened on green lawns outside. The Sector Chief, Sandringham, leaned back in a chair, smoking. Werner, the other summoned Senior Officer, sat bolt upright in a chair facing him. Sandringham waved a hand to Bordman.

"Back so soon? You're ahead of schedule on all counts! Here's Werner, back from looking at the fuel-store situation."

Bordman suddenly looked as if he'd been jolted. But he nodded, and Werner tried to smile and failed. He was completely white.

"My pilot from the ship, who's kept aground," said Bordman. "Lieutenant Barnes. Very promising young officer. Cut my landing-time by hours. Lieutenant, this is Sector Chief Sandringham and Mr. Werner."

"Have a seat, Bordman," grunted the Chief. "You too, Lieutenant. How does it look up on the cliff, Bordman?"

"I suspect you know as well as I do," said Bordman. "I think I saw a vision-camera planted up there."

"True enough. But there's nothing like on-the-spot inspection. Now you're back, how does it look to you?"

"Inadequate," said Bordman. "Inadequate to explain some things I've noticed. But it's a very bad situation. Its degree of badness depends on the viscosity of the mud at bedrock all over the island. The left-behind mud's like pea soup. It looks really bad! But what's the viscosity at bedrock with soil pressing down, and I hope more dried soil at the top than at the bottom?"

Sandringham grunted.

"Good question. I sent for you, Bordman, when it began to look bad, before the ground really started sliding. When I thought it might begin any time. The viscosity averages pretty closely at three times ten to the sixth. Which still gives us some leeway. But not enough."

"Not nearly enough!" said Bordman impatiently. "Irrigation should have been stopped a long while back!"

The Sector Chief grunted.

"I've no authority over civilians. They're their own planetary government. And do you remember?" He quoted: "'Civilian establishments and governments may be advised by Colonial Survey officials, and may make requests of them, but in each case such advice or request is to be considered on its own merits only, and in no case may be the subject of a *quid-pro-quo* agreement.'" He added grimly: "That means you can't threaten. It's been thrown at my head every time I've asked them to cut down their irrigation in the past fifteen years! I advised them not to irrigate at all, and they couldn't see it. It would increase the food-supply, and they needed more food. So they went ahead. They built two new seawater freshening plants only last year!"

Werner licked his lips. He said in a voice that was higher-pitched than Bordman remembered:

"What's happening serves them right! It serves them right!"

Bordman waited.

"Now," said Sandringham, "they're demanding to be let into Sector Headquarters for safety. They say we haven't irrigated, so the ground we occupy isn't going to slide. They demand that we take them all in here to sit on their rumps until the rest of the island slides into the sea or doesn't. If it doesn't, they want to wait here until the soil becomes stable again because they've quit irrigating."

"It'd serve them right if we let them in!" cried Werner in shrill anger. "It's their fault that they're in this fix!"

Sandringham waved his hand.

"Administering abstract justice isn't my job. I imagine it's handled in more competent quarters. I have only to meet the objective situation. Which is plenty! Bordman, you've handled swamp-planet situations. What can be done to stop the sliding of the island's soil before it all goes overboard?"

"Not much, offhand," said Bordman. "Give me time and I'll manage something. But a really bad storm, with high seas and plenty of rain, might wipe out the whole civilian colony. That viscosity figure is close to hopeless, if not quite."

The Sector Chief looked impassive.

"How much time does he have, Werner?"

"None!" said Werner shrilly. "The only possible thing is to try to move as many people as possible to the solid ground in the Arctic! The boats can be crowded — the situation demands it! And if the two space-craft in orbit are sent to collect a fleet, and as many people as possible are moved at once, there may be some survivors!"

Bordman spread out his hands.

"I'm wondering," he observed, "what the really serious problem is. There's more than sliding soil the matter! Else you would — I'm sure Lieutenant Barnes has thought of this — else you would let the civilian population into Headquarters to sit on its rump and wait for better times."

Sandringham glanced at young Barnes, who flushed hotly at being noticed.

"I'm sure you have good reasons, sir," he said, embarrassed.

"I have several," said the Sector Chief dryly. "For one thing, so long as we refuse to let them in, they're reassured. They can't imagine we'd let them drown. But if we invited them in they'd panic and fight to get in first. There'd be a full-scale slaughter right here! They'd be sure disaster was only minutes off. Which it would be!"

He paused and glanced from one to the other of the senior officers.

"When I sent for you," he said, "I meant you, Bordman, to take care of the possible sliding. I meant for Werner, here, to do the public-relations job of scaring the civilians just enough to make them let it be done. It's not so simple, now!"

He drew a deep breath.

"It's pure chance that this is a Sector Headquarters. Or else it's Providence. We'll find that out later! But ten days ago it was discovered that an instrument had gone wrong over in the ship-fuel storage area. It didn't register when a tank leaked. And a tank did leak. You know ship fuel is harmless when it's refrigerated.

You know what it's like when it's not. Dissolved in soil-moisture, it's not only catalyzed to explosive condition, but it's a hell of a corrosive, and it's eaten holes in some other tanks — and can you imagine trying to do anything about that?"

Bordman felt a sensation of incredulous shock. Werner wrung his hands.

"If I could only find the man who made that faulty tank!" he said thickly. "He's killed all of us! Unless we get to solid ground in the Arctic!"

The Sector Chief said:

"That's why I won't let them in, Bordman. Our storage tanks go down to bedrock. The leaked fuel — warmed up, now — is seeping along bedrock and eating at other tanks, besides being absorbed generally by the soil and dissolving in the ground-water. We've pulled all personnel out of all the area it could have seeped down to."

Bordman felt slightly cold at the back of his neck.

"I suspect," he said, "that they came out on tiptoe, holding their breaths, and they were careful not to drop anything or scrape their chairs when they got up to leave. I would have! Anything could set it off. But it is bound to go anyhow! Of course! Now I see why we couldn't make a rocket-landing!"

The chilly feeling seemed to spread as he realized more fully. When the ship-fuel is refrigerated during its manufacture, it is about as safe as a substance as can be imagined, so long as it is kept refrigerated. It is an energy-chemical compound, of atoms bound together with forced-valence linkages. But enormous amounts of energy are required to force valences upon reluctant atoms. When ship-fuel warms up, or is catalyzed, it goes on one step beyond the process of its manufacture. It goes on to the modification the refrigeration prevented. It changes its molecular configuration. What was stable because it was cold becomes something which is hysterically unstable because of its structure. The touch of a feather can detonate it. A shout can set it off. It is indeed, burned only molecule by molecule in a ship's engines, being catalyzed to the unstable state while cold at the very spot where it is to detonate. And since they energy yielded by detonation is that of the forced bonds, the energy-content of ship-fuel is much greater than a merely chemical compound can contain. Ship-fuel contains a measurable fraction of the power of atomic explosive. But it is much more practical for use on board ship.

The point now was, of course, that — leaked into the ground and warmed — practically any vibratory motion would detonate the fuel. Even dissolved, it can detonate because it is not a chemical but an energy-release action.

"A good, drumming, heavy rain," said Sandringham, "which falls on this end of the island, will undoubtedly set off some hundreds of tons of leaked ship-fuel. And that ought to scatter and catalyze and detonate the rest. The explosion should be equivalent to at least a megaton fusion bomb." He paused, and added with irony. "Pretty situation, isn't it? If the civilians hadn't irrigated, we could evacuate Headquarters and let it blow, as it will anyhow. If the fuel hadn't leaked, we could let in the civilians until the island's soil decides what it's going to do. Either would be a nasty situation, but the combination. . . ."

Werner said shrilly:

"Evacuation to the Arctic is the only possible answer! Some people can be saved! Some! I'll take a boat and equipment and go on ahead and make some sort of refuge ready —"

There was dead silence. The brown dog who had followed Bordman from the outer terrace now yawned loudly. Bordman reached over and absent-mindedly scratched his ears. Young Barnes swallowed.

"Beg pardon, sir," he said. "What's the weather forecast?"

"Continued fair," said Sandringham pleasantly. "That's why I had Bordman and Werner come down. Three heads are better than one. I've gambled their lives on their brains."

Bordman continued to scratch the brown dog's ears. Werner licked his lips. Young Barnes looked from one to another of them. Then he looked back at the Sector Chief.

"Sir," he said. "I — I think the odds are pretty good. Mr. Bordman, sir — he'll manage!"

Then he flushed hotly at his own presumption in saying something consoling to a Senior Chief. It was comparable to telling him how to top off his vacuum-suit tanks.

But the Sector Chief nodded in grave approval and turned to Bordman to hear what he had to say.

The leeward side of the island sloped gently into the water. From a boat offshore — say, a couple of miles out — the shoreline looked low and flat and peaceful. There were houses in view, and boats afloat. But they were much smaller than those that had been towing a twenty-mile-long oil-slick out to sea. These boats did not ply back and forth. Most of them seemed anchored. On some of them there was activity. Men went overboard, without splashing, and brought things up from the ocean bottom and dumped them inside the hulls. At long intervals men emerged from underwater and sat on the sides of the boats and smoked with an effect of leisure.

The sun shone, and the land was green, and a seeming of vast tranquility hung over the whole seascape. But the small Survey-personnel reaction-boat moved in toward the shore, and the look of things changed. At a mile, a mass of green that had seemed to be trees growing down to the water's edge became a thicket of tumbled trunks and overset branches where a tree-thicket had collapsed. At half a mile the water was opaque. There were things floating in it: the roof of a house, the leaves of an ornamental shrub, with nearby its roots showing at the surface, washed clean. A child's toy bobbed past the boat. It looked horribly pathetic. There were the exotic planes and angles of three wooden steps, floating in the ripples of the great ocean.

"Ignoring the imminent explosion of the fuel-store," said Bordman, "we need to find out something about what has to be done to the soil to stop its creeping. I hope you remembered, Lieutenant, to ask a great many useless questions."

"Yes, sir," said Barnes. "I tried to. I asked everything I could think of."

"Those boats yonder?"

Bordman indicated a boat from which something like a wire basket splashed into the water as he gestured.

"A garden-boat, sir," said Barnes. "On this side of the island the sea-bottom slopes so gradually that there are sea-gardens on the bottom. Shellfish from Earth do not thrive, sir, but there are edible sea-plants. The gardeners cultivate them as on land."

Bordman reached overside and carefully took his twentieth sample of the seawater. He squinted, and estimated the distance to shore.

"I shall try to imagine someone wearing a diving-mask and using a hoe," he said dryly. "What's the depth here?"

"We're half a mile out, sir," said Barnes. "It should be about sixty feet. The bottom seems to have about a three percent grade, sir. That's the angle of repose of the mud. There's no sand to make a steeper slope possible."

"Three percent's not bad!"

Bordman looked pleased. He picked up one of his earlier samples and tilted it, checking the angle at which the sediment came to rest. The bottom mud, here, was essentially the same as the soil of the land. But the soil of the land was definitely colloid. In seawater, obviously, it sank because of the salinity which made suspension difficult.

"You see the point, eh?" he asked. When Barnes shook his head, Bordman explained. "Probably for my sins I've had a good deal to do with swamp-planets. The mud of a salt-swamp is quite different from a freshwater swamp. The essential trouble with the people ashore is that by their irrigation they've contrived an island-wide swamp which happens to be upside down, the swamp at the bottom. So the question is, can it acquire the properties of a salt-swamp instead of a freshwater swamp without killing all the vegetation on the surface? That's why I'm after these samples. As we go inshore the water should be fresher, on a shallowing shore like this with drainage in this direction."

He gestured to the Survey private at the stern of the boat.

"Closer in, please."

Barnes said:

"Sir, motorboats are forbidden inshore. The vibrations."

Bordman shrugged.

"We will obey the rule. I've probably samples enough. How far out do the mudflats run, at the surface?"

"About two hundred yards at the surface, sir. The mud's about the consistency of thick cream. You can see where the ripples stop, sir."

Bordman stared. He turned his eyes away.

"Er — sir," said Barnes unhappily. "May I ask —?"

Bordman said dryly:

"You may. But the answer's pure theory. This information will do no good at all unless all the rest of the problem we face is solved. However, solving the rest of the problem will do no good if this part remains unsolved. You see?"

"Yes, sir. But the other parts seem more urgent."

Bordman shrugged.

There was a shout from a nearby boat. Men were pointing ashore. Bordman jerked his eyes to the shoreline.

A section of seemingly solid ground moved slowly toward the water. Its forefront seemed to disintegrate, and a slow-moving swell moved out over the rippleless border of the sea, where mudbanks like thick cream reached the surface.

The moving mass was a good half-mile in width. Its outer edge dissolved in the sea, and the top tilted, and green vegetation leaned downward and subsided into the water. It was remarkably like the way an ingot of non-ferrous metal slides into the pool made by its own melting.

But the aftermath was somehow horrifying. When the tumbled soil was dissolved and the grass undulated like a floating meadow on the water, there remained a jagged shallow gap in the land-bank. There were irregularities: vertical striations and un-evennesses in the exposed, broken soil.

Bordman snatched up glasses and put them to his eyes. The shore seemed to leap toward him. He saw the harsh outlines of the temporary cliff go soft. The bottom ceased to look like soil. It glistened. It moved outward in masses which grew rounded as they swelled. They flowed after the now-vanished fallen stuff, into the water. The top-soil was suddenly undercut. The wetter material under it flowed away, leaving a ledge which bore carefully tended flowering shrubs — Bordman could see specks of color which were their blossoms — and a brightly-colored, small, trim house in which some family had lived.

The flow-away of the deeper soil made a greater, more cavernous hollow beneath the surface. It began to collapse. The house teetered, fell, smashed. More soil dropped down, and more, and more.

Presently there was a depression, a sort of valley leading inland away from the sea, in what had been a rampart of green at the water's edge. It was still green, but through the glasses Bordman could see that trees had fallen, and a white-painted fence was splintered. And there was still movement.

The movement slowed and slowed, but it was not possible to say when it stopped. In reality, it did not stop. The island's soil was still flowing into the ocean.

Barnes drew a deep breath.

"I thought that was it, sir," he said shakily. "I mean — that the whole island would start sliding."

"The ground's a bit more water-soaked down here," Bordman said. "Inland the bottom-soil's not nearly as fluid as here. But I'd hate to have a really heavy rainfall right now!"

Barnes' mind jerked back to the Sector Chief's office.

"The drumming would set off the ship-fuel?"

"Among other things," said Bordman. "Yes." Then he said abruptly: "How good are you at precision measurements? I've messed around on swamp-planets. I know a bit too much about what I ought to find, which is not good for accuracy. Can you take these bottles and measure the rate of sedimentation and plot it against salinity?"

"Y-yes, sir. I'll try."

"If we had soil-coagulants enough," said Bordman, "we could handle that damned upside-down swamp the civilians have so carefully made here. But we haven't got it! The freshened seawater they've been irrigating with is practically mineral-free! I want to know how much mineral content in the water would keep the swamp-mud from acting like wet soap. It's entirely possible that we'd have to make the soil too salty to grow anything, in order to anchor it. But I want to know!"

Barnes said uncomfortably:

"Wouldn't you — wouldn't you have to put the minerals in irrigation-water to get them down to the swamp?"

Bordman grinned, surprisingly.

"You've got promise, Barnes! Yes, I would. And it would increase the rate of slide before it stopped it. Which could be another problem. But it was good work to think of it! When we get back to Headquarters, you commandeer a laboratory and make those measurements for me."

"Yes, sir," said Barnes.

"We'll start back now," said Bordman.

The recreation-boat obediently turned. It went out to sea until the water flowing past its hull was crystal-clear. And Bordman seemed to relax. On the way they passed more small boats. Many of them were gardeners' boats, from which men dived with diving-masks to tend or harvest the cultivated garden-patches not too far down. But many were pleasure-boats, from double-hulled sailing craft intended purely for sport, to sturdy, though small, cabin cruisers which could venture far out to sea, or even around to the windward of the island for sport-fishing. All the pleasure-craft were crowded — there were usually some children — and it was noticeable that on each on there were always some faces turned toward the shore.

"That," said Bordman, "makes for emotional thinking. These people know their danger. So they've packed their children and their wives into these little cockleshells to try to save them. They're waiting offshore here to find out if they're doomed regardless. I wouldn't say —" He nodded toward a delicately designed twin-hull sailer with more children than adults aboard — "I wouldn't call that a good substitute for an Ark!"

Young Barnes fidgeted. The boat turned again and went parallel to the shore toward where Headquarters land came down to the sea. The ground was firmer there. There had been no irrigation. Lateral seepage had done some damage at the end of the reserve, but the major part of the shoreline was unbroken, unchanged solid ground, looming above the beach. There was, of course, no sand at the edge of the water. There had been no weathering of rock to produce it. When this island was upraised, its coating of hardened ooze protected the stone, the lee-side waves merely lapped upon bare, curdled rock. The wharf for pleasure-boats went out on metal pilings into deep water.

"Excuse me, sir," said young Barnes, "but — if the fuel blows, it'll be pretty bad, won't it?"

"That's the understatement of the century," Bordman commented. "Yes. It will. Why?"

"You've something in mind to try to save the rest of the island. Nobody else seems to know what to do. If — if I may say so, sir, your safety is pretty important. And you could do your work on the cliffs, and — if I could stay at Headquarters and —"

He stopped, appalled at his own presumption in suggesting that he could substitute for a Senior Officer even as a message-boy, and even for his convenience or safety. He began to stammer:

"I m-mean, sir, n-not that I'm capable of it —"

"Stop stammering," grunted Bordman. "There aren't two separate problems. There's one which is the compound of the two. I'm staying at Headquarters to try something on the ship-fuel side, Werner will specialize on the rest of the island since he hasn't come up with anything but shifting people to the ice-pack. And the situation isn't hopeless! If there's an earthquake or a storm, of course, we'll be wiped out. But short of one of those calamities, we can save part of the island. I don't know how much, but some. You make those measurements. If you're doubtful, get a Headquarters man to duplicate them. Then give me both sets."

"Y-yes, sir," said young Barnes.

"And," said Bordman, "never try to push your ranking officer into a safe place, even if you're willing to take his risk! Would you like it if a man under you tried to put you in a safe place while he took the chance that was yours?"

"N-no, sir!" admitted the very junior lieutenant. "But —"

"Make those measurements!" snapped Bordman.

The boat came into the dock. Bordman got out and went to Sandringham's office.

Sandringham was in the act of listening to somebody in the phone-screen, who apparently was on the thin edge of hysteria. The brown dog was sprawled asleep on the rug.

When the man in the vision-screen panted to a stop, Sandringham said calmly:

"I am assured that before the soil of the island is too far gone, measures now in preparation will be applied to good effect. A Senior Survey Officer is now preparing remedial measures. He is — ah — a specialist in problems of exactly this nature."

"But we can't wait!" panted the civilian fiercely. "I'll proclaim a planetary emergency! We'll take over the reserve area by force! We have to —"

"If you try," Sandringham told him grimly, "I'll mount paralysis-guns to stop you!" He said with icy precision: "I urged the planetary government to go easy on this irrigation! You yourself denounced me in the Planetary Council for trying to interfere in civilian affairs. Now you want to interfere in Survey affairs! I resent it as much as you did, and with much better reason!"

"Murderer!" panted the civilian. "Murderer!"

Sandringham snapped off the phone-screen. He swung his chair and nodded to Bordman.

"That was the planetary president," he said.

Bordman sat down. The brown dog blinked his eyes open and then got up and shook himself.

"I'm holding off those idiots!" said the Sector Chief in suppressed fury. "I daren't tell him it's more dangerous here than outside! If or when that fuel blows — do you realize that the falling of a single tree-limb might set off an explosion in the Reserve-area here that would — But you do know."

"Yes," admitted Bordman.

He did know. Some hundreds of tons of ship-fuel going off would destroy this entire end of the island. And almost certainly the concussion would produce violent movement of the rest of the island's surface. But he was uncomfortable about putting forward his own ideas. He was not a good salesman. He suspected his own opinions until he had proved them with painstaking care, for fear of having them adopted on his post record rather than because they were sound. And then, too, this plan involved junior ranks being informed about the proposal. If they accepted a dubious plan on high authority, and the plan miscarried, it made them share in the mistake. Which hurt their self-confidence. Young Barnes, now, would undoubtedly obey any order and accept any hint blindly, and Bordman honestly did not know why. But as a matter of the training of junior ranks —

"About the work to be done," said Bordman, "I imagine the seawater freshening plants have closed down?"

"They have!" said Sandringham. "They insisted on piling them up over my protests. Now if anybody proposed operating one, they'd scream to high heaven!"

"What was done with the minerals taken out of the seawater?" Bordman asked.

"You know how the fresheners work!" said Sandringham. "They pump seawater in at one end, and at the other one pipe yields fresh water, and the other heavy brine. They dump the heavy brine back overboard and the fresh water's pumped up and distributed through the irrigation systems."

"It's too bad some of the salts weren't stored," said Bordman. "Could a freshener be started up again?"

Sandringham stared. Then he said:

"Oh, the civilians would love that! No! If any man started up a water-freshener, the civilians would kill him and smash it!"

"But I think we'll need one. We'll want to irrigate some of the Reserve area."

"My God! What for?" demanded Sandringham. He paused. "No! Don't tell me! Let me try to work it out."

There was silence. The dog blinked at Bordman. He held out his hand. The dog came sedately to him and bent his head to be scratched.

After a considerable time, the Sector Chief growled:

"I give up. Do you want to tell me?"

Bordman nodded. He said:

"In a sense, the trouble is that there's a swamp underground, made by irrigation. It slides. It's really a swamp upside down. On Soris II we had a very odd problem, only the swamp was right-side-up there. We'd several hundred square miles of swamp that could be used if we could drain it. We built a soil-dam around it. You know the trick. You bore two rows of holes twenty feet apart and put soil-coagulant in them. It's an old, old device. They used it a couple of hundred years back on Earth. The coagulate seeps out in all directions and coagulates the dirt. Makes it watertight. It swells with water and fills the spaces between with soil-particles. In a week or two there's a watertight barrier, made of soil, going down to bedrock. You might call it a coffer-dam. No water can seep through. On Soris II we knew that if we could get the water out of the mud inside this coffer-dam, we'd have cultivable ground."

Sandringham said skeptically:

"But it called for ten years' pumping, eh? When mud doesn't move, pumping is easy!"

"We wanted the soil," said Bordman. "And we didn't have ten years. The Soris II colony was supposed to relieve population-pressure on another planet. The pressure was terrific. We had to be ready to receive some colonists in eight months. We had to get the water out quicker than it could be pumped. And there was another problem mixed up with it. The swamp vegetation was pretty deadly. It had to be gotten rid of, too. So we made the dam and — well — took certain measures, and then we irrigated it. But we had dry ground in four months, with the swamp-vegetation killed and turning back to humus."

"I ought to read your reports," said Sandringham dourly. "I'm too busy, ordinarily. But I should read them. How'd you get rid of the water?"

Bordman told him. The telling required eighteen words.

"Of course," he added, "we picked a day when there was a strong wind from the right quarter."

Sandringham stared at him. Then he said:

"But how does that apply here? It was sound enough, though I'd never have thought of it. But what's it got to do with the situation here?"

"This swamp, you might say," said Bordman, "is underground. But there's forty feet, on an average, of soil on top."

He explained what difference that made. It took his three sentences to make the difference clear.

Sandringham leaned back in his chair. Bordman scratched the dog, somewhat embarrassed. Sandringham thought.

"I do not see any possible chance," said Sandringham distastefully, "of doing it any other way. I would never have thought of that! But I'm taking part of the job out of your hands, Bordman."

Bordman said nothing. He waited.

"Because," said Sandringham, "you're not the man to put over to the civilians what they must believe. You're not impressive. I know you, and I know you're a good man in a pinch. But this pinch needs a salesman. So I'm going to have Werner make the — er — pitch to the planetary government. Results are more important than justice, so Werner will front this affair."

Bordman winced a little. But Sandringham was right. He didn't know how to be impressive. He could not speak with pompous conviction, which is so much more convincing than reason to most people. He wasn't the man to get the cooperation of the non-Service population, because he could only explain what he knew and believed, and was not practiced in persuasion. But Werner was. He had the knack of making people believe anything not because it was reasonable but because it was oratory.

"I suppose you're right," acknowledged Bordman. "We need civilian help and a lot of it. I'm not the man to get it. He is." He did not say anything about Werner being the man to get credit, whether he deserved it or not. He patted the dog's head and stood up. "I wish I had a good supply of soil-coagulant. I need to make a coffer-dam in the reserve area here. But I think I'll manage."

Sandringham regarded him soberly as he moved to the door. As he was about to pass out of it, Sandringham said:

"Bordman —"

"What?"

"Take good care of yourself. Will you?"

Therefore Senior Officer Werner, of the Council Survey, received his instructions from Sandringham. Bordman never knew the details of the instructions Werner got. They were possibly persuasive, or they may have been menacing. But Werner ceased to argue for the movement of any fraction of the island's population to the arctic ice-cap, and instead made frequent eloquent addresses to the planetary population on the scientific means by which their lives were to be saved. Between the addresses, perhaps, he sweated cold sweat when a tree sedately tilted in what had seemed solid soil, or a building settled perceptibly while he looked at it, or when a section of the island's soil bulged upward.

Instead, he headed citizens' committees, and grandly gave instructions, and spoke in unintelligible and therefore extremely scientific terms when desperately earnest men asked for explanations. But he was perfectly clear in what he wanted them to do.

He wanted drill-holes in the arable soil down to the depth at which the holes began to close up of themselves. He wanted those holes not more than a hundred feet apart in lines which slanted at a little less than forty-five degrees to the gradient of the bedrock.

Sandringham checked his speeches, at the rate of four a day. Once he had Bordman called away from where he supervised some improbable operations. Bordman was smeared with the island's grayish mud when he looked into the phone-plate to take the call.

"Bordman," said Sandringham curtly. "Werner's saying those holes you want are to be in lines exactly forty-five degrees to the gradient."

"That — I'd like a little less," said Bordman. "If they slanted three miles across the grade for every two downhill, it would be better. I'd like to put a lot more lines of holes. But there's the element of time."

"I'll have to explain that he was misquoted," said Sandringham, grimly. "Three across to two down. How close do you really want those lines?"

"As close as possible," said Bordman. "But I've got to have them quickly. How does the barometer look?"

"Down a tenth," said Sandringham.

Bordman said:

"Damn! Has he got plenty of labor?"

"All the labor there is," said Sandringham. "And I'm having a road laid along the cliffs for speed with the trucks. If I dared — and if I had the pipe — I'd lay a pipe-line."

"Later," said Bordman tiredly. "If he's got labor to spare, set them to work turning the irrigation systems hind part before. Make them drainage systems. Use pumps. So if rain does come it won't be spread out on the land by all the pretty ditches. So it will be gathered instead of either flung back over the cliffs or else drained downhill without getting a chance to sink into the ground. For the time being, anyhow."

Sandringham said:

"Has it occurred to you what a good, pounding rain would do to Headquarters, and consequently to public confidence on this island, and therefore to the attempt of anybody to do anything but wring his hands because he was doomed?"

Bordman grimaced.

"I'm irrigating, here. I've got a small-sized lake made, and an ice coffer-dam, and the water-freshener is working around the clock. If there is labor, tell 'em to fix the irrigation systems into draining layouts. That'd cheer them, anyhow."

He was very weary. There is a certain exhausting quality in the need to tell other men to do work which may cause them to be killed. The fact that one would certainly be killed with them did not lessen the tension.

He went back to his work. And it definitely seemed to be as purposeless as any man's work could possibly be. Down-grade from the now thoroughly deserted area in which ship-fuel tanks had leaked — quite far down-grade — he had commandeered all the refrigeration equipment in the warehouses. Since refrigeration was necessary for fuel-storage, there was a great deal. He had planted iron pipes in the soil, and circulated refrigerant in it. Presently there was a wall of solidly frozen soil which was shaped like a hollow U. In the curved part of that U he'd siphoned out a lake. A peristaltic pump ran seawater from the island's lee out upon the ground — where it instantly turned to mud — and another peristaltic pump sucked the mud up again and delivered it down-grade beyond the line of freezing-pipes. It was in fact a system of hydraulic dredging such as is normally performed in rivers and harbors. But when top-soil is merely former abyssal mud it is an excellent way to move dirt. Also, it does not require anybody to strike blows into soil which may be explosive when one has gotten down near bedrock, and in particular there are no clanking machines.

But it was hair-raising.

In one day, though, he had a sizeable lake pumped out. And he pumped it out to emptiness, smelling the water as it went down to a greater depth below the previous ground surface. At the end of the day he shivered and ordered pumping ended for the time.

Then he had a brine-pipe laid around a great circuit, to the Headquarters ground which was up-grade from the now-deserted square mile or so in which the fuel-tanks lay deep in the soil. And here, also, he performed excavation without the sound of hammer, shovel, or pick. He thrust pipes into the ground, and they had nozzles at the end which threw part of the water backward. So that when seawater poured into them it thrust them deeper into the ground by the backward jet action. Again the fact that the soil was abyssal mud made it possible. The nozzles floated up much grayish mud, but they bored ahead down to bed-rock, and there they lay flat and tunneled to one side and the other, the tunnels they made being full of water at all times.

From those tunnels, as they extended, an astonishing amount of seawater seeped out into the soil near bedrock. But it was seawater. It was heavily mineralized. It is a peculiarity of seawater that it is an electrolyte, and it is a property of electrolytes that they coagulate colloids, and discourage the suspension of small solid particles which are on the borderline of being colloids. In fact, the water of the ocean of Canna III turned the ground-soil into good, honest mud which did not feel at all soapy, and through which it percolated with a surprising readiness.

Young Barnes supervised this part of the operation, once it was begun. He shamed the Survey personnel assigned to him into perhaps excessive self-confidence.

"He knows what he's doing," he said firmly. "Look here! I'll take that canteen. It's fresh water. Here's some soap. Wet it in fresh water and it lathers. See? It dissolves. Now try to dissolve it in seawater! Try it! See? They put salt in the boiled stuff to separate the soap out, when they make it!" He picked up that item from Bordman. "Seawater won't soften the ground. It can't! Come on, now, let's get another pipe putting more salt water underground!"

His workmen did not understand what he was doing, but they labored willingly because it was for a purpose. . . . And downhill, in the hydraulic-dredged-out lake, water came seeping in, in the form of mud. And another pipe came up from the seashore. It was a rather small pipe, and the personnel who laid it were bewildered. Because there was a water-freshening plant down there and all the fresh water was poured back overboard, while the brine, saturated with salts from the ocean, unable to dissolve a single grain of anything, was being used to fill the small artificial lake.

The second day Sandringham called Bordman again, and again Bordman peered wearily into the phone-screen.

"Yes," said Bordman. "The leaked fuel is turning up. In solution. I'm trying to measure the concentration by matching specific gravities of lake-water and brine, and then sticking electrodes in each. The fuel's corrosive as the devil. It gives a different EMF. Higher than brine of the same density. I think I've got it in hand."

"Do you want to start shipping it?" demanded Sandringham.

"You can begin pouring it down the holes," said Bordman. "How's the barometer?"

"Down three-tenths this morning. Steady now."

"Damn!" said Bordman. "I'll set up moulds. Freeze it in plastic bags the size of bore-holes so it will go down. While it's frozen they can even push it down deep."

Sandringham said grimly:

"There's been more damned technical work done with ship-fuel than any other substance since time began. But remember that the stuff can still be set off, even dissolved in water! Its sensitivity goes down, but it's not gone!"

"If it were," said Bordman drearily, "you could invite in the civilian population to sit on its rump. I've got something like forty tons of ship-fuel in brine solution in this lake I pumped out! But it's in five thousand tons of brine. We don't speak above a whisper when we're around it. We walk in carpet-slippers and you never saw people so polite! We'll start freezing it."

"How can you handle it?" demanded Sandringham apprehensively.

"The brine freezes at minus thirty," said Bordman. "In one percent solution it's only five percent sensitive at minus nineteen. We're handling it at minus nineteen. I think I'll step up the brine and chill it a little more."

He waved a mud-smeared hand and went away.

That day, bolster-trucks began to roll out of Survey Headquarters. They rolled very smoothly, and they trailed a fog of chilled air behind them. And presently there were men with heavy gloves on their hands taking long things like sausages out of the bolster-trucks and untying the ends and lowering them down into holes bored in the topsoil until they reached places where wetness made the holes close up again. Then the men from Survey pushed those frozen sausages underground still further by long poles with carefully padded — and refrigerated ends. And then they went on to other holes.

The first day there were five hundred such sausages thrust down into holes in the ground, which holes to all intents and purposes closed up behind them. The second day there were four thousand. The third day there were eight. On the fourth the solution of ship-fuel in brine in the lake was so thin that it did not give enough EMF in the little battery-cell to show how much corrosive substance there was in the brine. It was not mud any longer. Brine flowed at the top of bedrock, and it left the mud behind it, because salt water hindered the suspension of former globigerinous ooze particles. It was practically colloid. Saltwater almost coagulated it.

The brine flowing from the saltwater tunnels upwind showed no more ship-fuel in it. Bordman called Sandringham and told him.

"I can call in the civilians," said Sandringham. "You've mopped up the leaked stuff! It couldn't have been done —"

"Not anywhere but here with bedrock handy just underneath and slanting," admitted Bordman. "Tell them they can come if they want to. They'll sort of drift in. I want to top some more ship-fuel for the rest of those bore-holes."

Sandringham hesitated.

"Twenty thousand holes," said Bordman tiredly. "Each one had a six-hundred pound block of frozen saturated brine dumped in it with roughly a pound of ship-fuel in solution. We've gone that far. Might as well go the rest of the way. How's the barometer?"

"Up a tenth," said Sandringham. "Still rising."

Bordman blinked at him, because he had trouble keeping his eyes open.

"Let's ride it, Sandringham!"

Sandringham hesitated. Then he said:

"Go ahead."

Bordman waved his arms at his associates, whom he admired with great fervor in his then-foggy mind, because they were always ready to work when it was needed, and it had not stopped being needed for five days running. He explained that there was only three more miles of holes to be filled up, and therefore they would just draw so much of ship-fuel and blend it carefully with an appropriate amount of chilled brine and then freeze it in appropriate sausages. . . .

Young Lieutenant Barnes said:

"Yes, sir. I'll take care of it."

Bordman said:

"Barometer's up a tenth." His eyes did not quite focus. "All right, Lieutenant. Go ahead. Promising young officer. Excellent. I'll sit down here for just a moment."

When Barnes came back, Bordman was asleep. And a last one hundred and fifty frozen sausages of brine and ship-fuel went out of Headquarters within a matter of hours. Then a vast quietude settled down everywhere.

Young Barnes sat beside Bordman, menacing anybody who even thought of disturbing him. When Sandringham called for him Barnes went to the phone-plate.

"Sir," he said with vast formality. "Mr. Bordman went five days without sleep. His job's done. I won't wake him, sir!"

Sandringham raised an eyebrow.

"You won't?"

"I won't, sir!" said young Barnes.

Sandringham nodded.

"Fortunately," he observed, "nobody's listening. You are quite right."

He snapped the connection. And then young Barnes realized that he had defied a Sector Chief, which is something distinctly more improper in a junior officer than merely trying to instruct him in topping off his vacuum-suit tanks.

Twelve hours later, however, Sandringham called for him.

"Barometer's dropping, Lieutenant. I'm concerned. I'm issuing a notice of the impending storm. Not everybody will crowd in on us, but a great many will. I'm explaining that the chemicals put into the bottom soil may not quite have finished their work. If Bordman wakens, tell him."

"Yes, sir," said Barnes.

But he did not intend to wake Bordman. Bordman, however, woke of himself at the end of twenty hours of sleep. He was still and sore and his mouth tasted as if something had kittened in it. Fatigue can produce a hangover, too.

"How's the barometer?" he asked when his eyes came open.

"Dropping, sir. Heavy winds. The Sector Chief has opened the Reserve Area to the civilians if they wish to come."

Bordman computed dizzily on his fingers. A more complex instrument was actually needed, of course. One does not calculate on one's fingers just how long a one percent dilute solution of ship-fuel in frozen brine has taken to melt, and how completely it has diffused through an upside-down swamp with the pressure of forty feet of soil on top of it, and therefore its effective concentration and dispersal underground.

"I think," said Bordman, "it's all right. By the way, did they turn the irrigation system hind end to?"

Young Barnes did not know what this was all about. He had to send for information. Meanwhile he solicitously plied Bordman with coffee and food. Bordman grew reflective.

"Queer," he said. "You think of the damage leaked ship-fuel can do. Setting off the rest of the stone and all. Even by itself it rates some thousands of tons of TNT. I wonder what TNT was, before it became a ton-measure of energy? You think of it exploding in one place, and it's appalling! But think of all that same amount of energy applied to square miles of upside-down swamp. Hundreds or thousands of miles of upside-down swamp. D'you know, Lieutenant, on Soris II we pumped a ship-fuel solution onto a swamp we wanted to drain? Flooded it, and let it soak until a day came with a nice, strong, steady wind."

"Yes, sir," said Barnes respectfully.

"Then we detonated it. We didn't have a one percent solution. It was more like a thousandth of one percent solution. Nobody's ever measured the speed of propagation of an explosion of ship-fuel, dry. But it's been measured in dilute solution. It isn't the speed of sound. It's lower. It's purely a temperature-phenomenon. In water, at any dilution, ship-fuel goes off just barely below the boiling point of water. It doesn't detonate from shock when it's diluted enough to be ionized, but that takes a hell of a lot of dilution. Have you got some more coffee?"

"Yes, sir," said Barnes. "Coming up."

"We floated ship-fuel solution over that swamp, Barnes, and let it stand. It has a high diffusion-rate. It went down into the mud . . . And there came a day when the wind was right. I dumped a red-hot iron into the swamp-water that had ship-fuel in solution. It was the damndest sight you ever saw!"

Barnes served him more coffee. Bordman sipped it, and it burned his tongue.

"It went up in steam," he said. "The swamp-water that had the ship-fuel dissolved in it. It didn't explode, as a mass. They told me later that it propagated at hundreds of feet per second only. They could see a wall of steam go marching across the swamp. Not even high-pressure steam. There was a whoosh! and a cloud of steam half a mile high that the wind carried away. And all the surface-water in the swamp was gone, and all the poisonous swamp-vegetation parboiled and dead. So —" He yawned suddenly — "we had a ten-mile by fifty-mile stretch of arable ground ready for the coming colonists."

He tried the coffee again. He added reflectively:

"That trick, it didn't explode the ship-fuel, in a way. It burned it. In water. It applied the energy of the fuel to the boiling-away of water. Powerful stuff! We got rid of two feet of water on an average, counting what came out of the mud. It cost — hm — a fraction of a gram per square yard."

He gulped the coffee down. There were men looking at him solicitously. They seemed very glad to see him awake again. Outside a monstrous bank of cloud-stuff was visibly piling up in the sky. He suddenly blinked at that.

"Hello! How long did I sleep, Barnes?"

Barnes told him. Bordman shook his head to clear it.

"We'll go see Sandringham," said Bordman. "I'd like to postpone firing as long as I can, short of having the stuff start draining into the sea to leeward."

Several mud-stained men were standing around the place where Bordman had slept. When he went, still groggy, out to the bolster-truck young Barnes had waiting, they regarded Bordman in a very respectful manner. Somebody grunted, "Good to have worked with you, sir," which is about as much of admiration as anybody would want to hear expressed. These associates of Bordman in the mopping-up of leaked ship's fuel would be able to brag of the job at all times and in all places hereafter.

Then the truck went trundling away in search of Sandringham.

It found him on the cliffs to the windward side of the island. The sea was no longer a cerulean blue. It was slaty-color. There were occasional flecks of white foam on the water four thousand feet below. There were dark clouds, by then covering practically all the sky. Far out to sea, there were small craft heading for the ends of the island, to go around it and ride out the coming storm in its lee.

Sandringham greeted Bordman with relief. Werner stood close by, opening and closing his hands jerkily.

"Bordman!" said the Sector Chief cordially. "We're having a disagreement, Werner and I. He's confident that the turning of the irrigation systems hind end to — making them surface-draining systems, in effect — will take care of the whole situation. Adding the brine underground, he thinks, will have done a good deal more. He says it'll be bad, psychologically, for anything more to be done. He didn't speak of it, and it would injure public confidence in the Survey."

Bordman said curtly:

"The only thing that will make a permanent difference on this island is for the water-fresheners to be a little less efficient. Barnes has the figures. He computed them from some measurements I had him make. If the water-freshener plants don't take all the sea-minerals out; if they don't make the irrigation water so infernally soft and suitable for hair-washing and the like; if they turn out hard water for irrigation, this won't happen again. But there's too much water underground now. We've got to get it out, because a little more's going underground from this storm, surface-drainage systems or no surface-drainage systems."

Sandringham pointed to leeward, where a black, thick procession of human beings trooped toward the Survey area on foot and by every possible type of vehicle.

"I've ordered them turn into the ship-sheds and warehouses," said the Sector Chief. "But of course we haven't shelter for all of them. At a guess, when they feel safe they'll go back to their homes even through the storm."

The sky to windward grew darker and blacker. There was no longer a steady flow of wind coming over the cliff's edge. It came in gusts, now, of extreme violence. They could make a man stagger on his feet. There were more flecks of white on the ocean's surface.

"The boats," added Sandringham, "were licked. There simply wasn't enough oil to maintain the slick. The radio reports were getting hysterical before I ordered them told that we had it beaten on shore. They're running for shelter now. I think they'd have stayed out there trying to hold the slick in place with their towline, if I hadn't said we had matters in hand."

Werner said, tight-lipped:

"I hope we have!"

Bordman shrugged.

"The wind's good and strong, now," he observed. "Let's find out. You've got the starting system all set?"

Sandringham waved his hand toward a high-voltage battery. It was of a type designed for blasting on airless planets, but the did not matter. Its cables led snakily for a couple of hundred feet to a very small pile of grayish soil which had been taken out of a bore-hole, and went over that untidy heap and down into the ground. Bordman took hold of the firing-handle. He paused.

"How about the highways?" he asked. "There might be some steam out of this hole."

"All allowed for," said Sandringham. "Go ahead."

There was a gust of wind strong enough to blow a man down, and a humming sound in the air, as wind beat upon the four-thousand foot cliff and poured over its top. There were gradually rising waves, below. The sky was gray, the sea slate-colored. Far, far to windward, the white line of pouring rain upon the water came marching toward the island.

Bordman pumped the firing-handle.

There was a pause, while wind-gusts tore at his garments and staggered him where he stood. It was quite a long pause.

Then a vapor came jetting out of the bore-hole. It was perfectly white. It came out with a sudden burst which was not in any sense explosive, but was merely a vast rushing of vaporized water. Then, a hundred yards away, there was a mistiness on the grassy surface. Still farther, a crack in the surface-soil let out a curtain of white vapor.

Here and there, everywhere, gouts of steam poured into the air and tumbled into the storm-wind. It was noticeable that the steam did not come out as an invisible vapor and condense in mid-air. It poured out of the ground in clouds, already condensed but thrust out by more masses of vapor behind it. It was not super-heated steam that came out. It was simply steam. Harmless steam, like the stream out of the spouts of teakettles. It rose from individual places everywhere. It made a massive coating of vapor which the storm-wind blew away. In seconds a half-mile of soil was venting steam. In seconds more a mile. The thick fleecy vapor swept across the landscape. The storm-wind could only tumble it and sweep it away.

In minutes there was no part of the island to be seen at all, save only the thin line of the cliffs reaching away between dark water on the one hand and snow-white clouds of vapor on the other.

"It can't scald anybody, can it?" asked Barnes uneasily.

"Not," said Bordman, "when it's had to come up through forty feet of soil. It's been pretty well cooled off in taking up some extra moisture. It spreads pretty well, doesn't it?"

The Sector Chief's office had tall windows — doors, really — that looked out upon green lawn and many trees. Now sheets of rain beat down outside. Wind whipped at the trees. There was tumult and roaring and vibration of gusts of hurricane force. Even the building in which the Sector Chief's office was vibrated slightly in the wind.

The Sector Chief beamed. The brown dog came in, looked around the room, and walked in leisurely fashion toward Bordman. He settled with a sigh beside Bordman's chair.

"What I want to know," said Werner, "is, won't this rain put back all the water the ship-fuel boiled away?"

Bordman said:

"Two inches of rain would be a heavy fall, Sandringham tells me. It's the lack of heavy rains that made the civilians start irrigating. When you figure the energy-content of ship-fuel, Werner, an appreciable fraction of the energy in atomic explosive, it's sort of deceptive. Turn it into thermal units and it gets to be enlightening. We turn loose, underground, enough heat to boil away two feet of soil-water under the island's whole surface."

Werner said sharply:

"What'll happen when the heat passes up through the soil? It'll kill the vegetation, won't it?"

"No," said Bordman mildly. "Because there was two feet of water to be turned to steam. The bottom layer of the soil was raised to the temperature of steam at a few pounds pressure. No more. The heat's already escaped. In the steam."

The phone-plate lighted. Sandringham snapped it on. A voice made a report in a highly official voice.

"Right!" said Sandringham. The highly official voice spoke again. "Right!" said Sandringham again. "You may tell the ships in orbit that they can come down now, if they don't mind getting wet." He turned. "Did you hear that, Bordman? They've bored new cores. There are a few soggy spots, but the ground's as firm, all over the island, as it was when the Survey first came here. A very good job, Bordman! A very good job!"

Bordman flushed. He reached down and patted the head of the brown dog.

"Look!" said the Sector Chief. "My dog, there, has taken a liking to you. Will you accept him as a present, Bordman?"

Bordman grinned.

Young Barnes made ready to rejoin his ship. He was very strictly Service, very stiffly at attention. Bordman shook hands with him.

"Nice to have had you around, Lieutenant," he said warmly. "You're a very promising young officer. Sandringham knows it and has made a note of the fact. Which I suspect is going to put you to a lot of trouble. There's a devilish shortage of promising young officers. He'll give you hellish jobs to do, because he has an idea you'll do them."

"I'll try, sir," said young Barnes formally. Then he said, "May I say something, sir? I'm very proud to have worked with you. But dammit, sir, it seems to me that something more than just saying thank you was due you! The Service ought to —"

Bordman regarded the young man approvingly.

"When I was your age," he said, "I'd the very same attitude. But I had the only reward the Service or anything else could give me. The job is done. It's the only reward you can expect in the Service, Barnes. You'll never get any other."

Young Barnes looked rebellious. He shook hands again.

"Besides," said Bordman, "there is no better."

Young Barnes marched back toward his ship in the great metal crisscross of girders which was the landing-grid.

Bordman absently patted his dog as he headed back toward Sandringham's office for his orders to return to his own work.

So Bordman went back to his wife Riki and the job he'd been working on. After that there was another job, and another. He received the high honor of being given the most impossible of the tasks the Survey was forced to do. Which was deeply satisfying. He regretted that he had to become relatively inactive when he became Sector Chief.

But his wife liked it very much. There was assurance, then, that they would be together for always, and Bordman still had his work and she could make — again — a home. When one of his daughters was widowed and came to live with them with her children, Bordman was beautifully contented. Then he had absolutely everything he wanted. As reward for a lifetime of work and separation, he had the satisfaction — in his family — that other men enjoyed as a matter of course.

But sometimes he was embarrassed when his juniors were too respectful. He didn't think he rated it.

THE END

www.ingramcontent.com/pod-product-compliance
Lightning Source LLC
Chambersburg PA
CBHW052141170626
46812CB00004B/1541